A Child's Seasonal Treasury

A Child's Seasonal Treasury

Compiled and Written by Betty Jones

TRICYCLE PRESS
Berkeley, California

MUSIC PERMISSIONS

In the Garden—Seasons and Festivals; Mealtime Blessing Songs; Sing and Do; Midwinter Night; Earth, Sun, Wind & Rain; Lady Spring; and *Midsummer Garden* are all from the Wynstones Press Kindergarten Book Series. Copyright © 1983 by Wynstones Press. Reprinted by permission of Wynstones Press. Special thanks to Peter Patterson for the music for *In the Garden—Seasons and Festivals* and *Earth, Sun, Wind & Rain.*

Special thanks to Margret Meyerkort for all her kind assistance and specifically for use of *In the Garden—Seasons and Festivals; Mealtime Blessing Songs; Sing and Do; When Mary Goes Walking; Midwinter Night;* and *Lady Spring.*

PERMISSIONS

Flower Elves; Woodchoppers; Morning; Go, My Pony, Go; My Horses; Little Birdie; Little Fish; Big Cow; The River; Birthday Anticipation; Morning Verse; Working Gnomes; Chestnuts; The Northwind; and *The Rain* are all from the Kindergarten Book Series. Copyright © 1983 by Wynstones Press. Reprinted by permission of Wynstones Press.

Bee Hive by Emily Poullson. Copyright © 1971 by Dover Publishing, Inc. Reprinted by permission of Dover Publishing, Inc.

Learning to Knit by Joan Marcus and *The Little Plant* by Kate Louise Brown are both from *And Then Take Hands.* Copyright © 1981 by Celestial Arts. Reprinted by permission of Celestial Arts.

The Sun Says by Eileen Hutchins is from *Come unto These Yellow Sands.* Copyright © 1984 by Steiner Schools Fellowship. Reprinted by permission of Molly von Heider, Steiner Schools Fellowship.

If, Five Little Peas, Pussy Willow, Five Little Seeds, Fish Alive, The Sea, The Elephant, Visit to a Farm, Movement Game, Two Little Blackbirds, The Golden Boat, Five Little Leaves, Little Brown Rabbit, and *The Apple Tree* are all from *This Little Puffin,* compiled by Elizabeth Matterson. Copyright © 1969 by Puffin Books. Reproduced by permission of Penguin Books Ltd.

Cleaning Up, Coloring Verse, Snowflakes, and *Waterfall Fairies* are all by Wendalyn von Meyenfeldt. Reprinted by permission of Wendalyn von Meyenfeldt.

The Lighted Candle and *May Day* are both from the Oxford Nursery Rhyme Book, assembled by Iona & Peter Opie. Copyright © 1955 by Oxford University Press (Claredon Press). Reprinted by permission of Oxford University Press.

Star Secrets by Margret Meyerkort. Copyright © 1983 by Wynstones Press. Reprinted by permission of Margret Meyerkort.

My Hands and *Bunny* are both taken from *Finger Plays.* Reprinted by permission of Mercury Press.

Number Verses and *Odd/Even Game* are both by Eugene Schwartz. Copyright © 1993 by Eugene Schartz. Reprinted by permission of Eugene Schwartz.

Whole Wheat Bread. Copyright © 1976 by Natural Recipes.

Early Morning by Hilaire Belloc has been used with expressed permission by the estate of Louis Untermeyer, Norma Anchin Untermeyer, c/o Professional Publishing Services.

Silver and *The Little Creature* by Walter de la Mare. Copyright © 1969 by The Society of Authors. Reprinted by permission of The Literary Trustees of Walter de la Mare, and The Society of Authors as their representative.

TRICYCLE PRESS
P.O. Box 7123
Berkeley, California 94707

Text and full-color illustrations copyright © 1996 by Betty Jones
Line illustrations © 1996 by Catherine Rose Crowther

Book design by Sarah Levin

CREDITS
All possible care has been taken to trace the ownership of every selection included in this book and to make full acknowledgment of its use. If any errors have inadvertently occurred, they will be corrected in subsequent editions, provided notification is sent to the publisher. Many of the pieces included here are traditional, with the author unknown. All known authors have been credited, and full credit is given on this page.

Library of Congress Cataloging-in-Publication Data
Jones, Betty M., 1952-
    A child's seasonal treasury / compiled and illustrated by
Betty M. Jones
        p.   cm.
    Includes index.
    ISBN 1-883672-30-9
    1. Creative activities and seatwork. 2. Early childhood
education—Activity programs. 3. Children's poetry.
4. Children's songs. 5. Waldorf method of education. I. Title.
LB1139.35.A37J66   1996
372.13—dc20   95-13190
                                                                                     CIP

Printed in Hong Kong.
2 3 4 5 6—01 00 99 98 97

Contents

Acknowledgments

Much of the material in this book originated from my study and work in Rudolf Steiner's Waldorf Education at Emerson College in England, and under the mentorship of Margret Meyerkort in the Wynstones School kindergarten during the mid-1970's. I am greatly indebted to Margret, as well as to Irene Ellis, a veteran Waldorf teacher. Irene helped pioneer a number of beginning Steiner schools in California and Oregon. Both these women have inspired many people world-wide to appreciate the needs of the growing child, and to apply the educational principles of Rudolf Steiner. Dr. Steiner, a prominent Austrian philosopher and scientist, founded the first Waldorf School in Stuttgart, Germany, for the workers' children of the Waldorf-Astoria Cigarette Factory. Seeking to bring to balance the imbalances of the post–World War I era, Steiner applied his insights regarding child development to a universally creative form of education. The Waldorf/Steiner schools have survived the tests of time and have grown to become the strongest international school movement. The role of this education is to guard the sanctity of childhood while guiding children through the developmental and learning stages appropriate to their ages.

The variety of my experiences working as a teacher and a therapist in both the Northern and Southern Hemispheres, in Waldorf and other alternative schools, as well as in the public school special education system, has made very clear to me the benefits of Waldorf education. Steiner's philosophy of education begins long before children enter school. His insights are valuable tools to the children's first teachers, their parents.

I encourage you to supplement this Treasury with the Wynstones Press Kindergarten Book Series. In addition, *Festivals, Family, and Food,* as well as *Festivals Together* and *The Children's Year* offer more details on the meaning of festivals, while presenting a wide array of handwork, crafts, cooking, and baking projects to share with children. The *Clarendon Book of Singing Games* is also highly recommended.

Thank you to all the wonderful writers whose work is compiled in this book. Whenever possible the author's name appears with their creation, however many of these pieces have been handed down through generations and their origins have been lost. If no author is indicated the piece is anonymous.

Further acknowledgment and deep gratitude go to Bruce and Jessica King for their help in the graphic layout and original editing of the manuscript. I very much appreciate their warmth of heart and hearth, and their constant encouragement. My appreciation goes to Don Lax for his musical transcription of my well-worn and faded original manuscripts, included here. And thanks to Connie Coleman for her music editing. To Paul Schraub and Ron Pierce I owe a debt of gratitude for their photography of old and new watercolor paintings. Many thanks are extended to Barbara Kane from Hearthsong, who saw the potential in my original teaching notes, paintings, and illustrations and co-edited the final copy with Molly Collum and Lynn Ostling. Heartfelt thanks to Nicole Geiger at Tricycle Press, from whom I have learned so much as she helped bring this work to final publication. Blessings to my godparents, Ray and Patty Miller, for their unwavering love and support; to my nieces, Aurora, Acacia, and Ryanda, on whom I practiced many of these activities; and to the many colleagues, children, and parents with whom I have worked and shared these wonderful treasures. These are gifts given from the hearts of many.

Introduction

This book contains the work of many talented teachers, poets, musicians, artists, and people creatively involved with children. It was inspired into being by the many parents with whom I have worked. They wanted to share in the joy and magic of their children's learning and provide home environments that protected, as much as possible, this tender time of childhood. Over the years as a teacher and a therapist, I have compiled this work of many into a Treasury of songs, verses, and creative activities to serve as a resource and inspiration to my own creative and therapeutic work. I now offer this Treasury to parents and teachers with my hope that it will be of practical use in your activities with children during their formative years, ideally from age two to age seven.

The seasonal format begins with "All Year Round" providing a foundation for the interweaving of the realms of Nature and the elemental world of fairies and gnomes. This allows the imagination to unfold, creating a joyful living and learning environment. Within this thematic structure, there is ample room for seasonal and cultural variation so that the children experience a genuine relationship with their natural environment, traditional festivals, and cultural heritage.

It is wonderful for families to share in festivals of many different cultures. We are fortunate today to have more and more opportunities to do so. Whenever seasonal and religious festivals are celebrated, it is best to have someone from that specific culture shepherding children through the proceedings. This will insure that they experience the traditional custom authentically.

When engaged in cooking, crafts, and movement activities, it is important to consider safety. As adults we must serve as role models, supervisors, and keen observers of the children in our care. Our attentions can safely provide children with the challenge to gain skills without being pushed to perform beyond their personal limits. Safety is further enhanced by the sense of security and familiarity that occurs when activities are brought with regular rhythms and patterns. These rhythms are created with the sharing of morning, evening, mealtime, and birthday verses, regular times for waking and sleeping, and particular daily activities like baking on Monday, painting on Tuesday, handwork on Wednesday, and so on. Children feel comfort in knowing what is coming next, and they experience joy in anticipation. Verses, songs, and poems which relate to the cycles of time and Nature bring balance and security to the child's existence. They instill thankfulness and wonder for life on Earth.

When we look at the growing child, we see a person who is only gradually moving into a familiarity with and understanding of the world where the great wonders of Nature can be experienced. By way of imitation, children initially learn about their physical abilities and functions. They grow into their life values and skills through their observations of adults. This is why it is so important that we do our best to provide models of behavior and values that are worthy of the child's innate faculty for imitation.

Movement, creative drama, and fingerplays engage the child's body and imagination while offering a joyful social interchange. Through gesture and movement interwoven with rhythm and rhyme, the child's sense of feeling and bodily expression is evoked and graceful agility enhanced.

Cooking and baking are social activities where Nature's gifts are transformed by human hands to create food to share. It is wonderful for children to experience the origin of the ingredients they use. Doing things like making at least part of the flour for a recipe by grinding wheatberries in a handmill gives children a true picture of the origins of the food they eat. Ideally this theme can be enhanced by providing children with a garden plot to share with the whole family a harvest of vegetables, flowers, and herbs. Visits to local dairies, farms, and gardens are excellent ways of meeting this need to experience origins.

Art and handwork activities delight children while they build skills. It is worthwhile to begin with raw, natural materials. You will see how the child's sense of color, form, and design blossom as their imagination unfolds.

Cooperative games and riddles engage the children socially and intellectually in a light-hearted frolic.

With the surge of home schools, daycare centers, preschools, and charter schools, the awareness to provide children with wholesome, enriching experiences is profound and the questions are many. I hope that this Treasury will serve as joyful resource and inspiration to parents and teachers. I offer it with the hope and intention of educating the Whole Child—giving each child the foundation for unfolding their unique selves in relation to Nature and humanity.

A Child's Seasonal Treasury

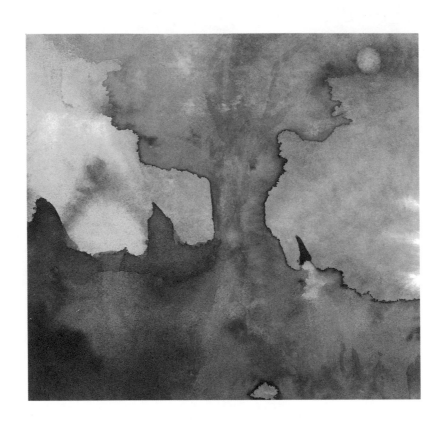

All Year Round

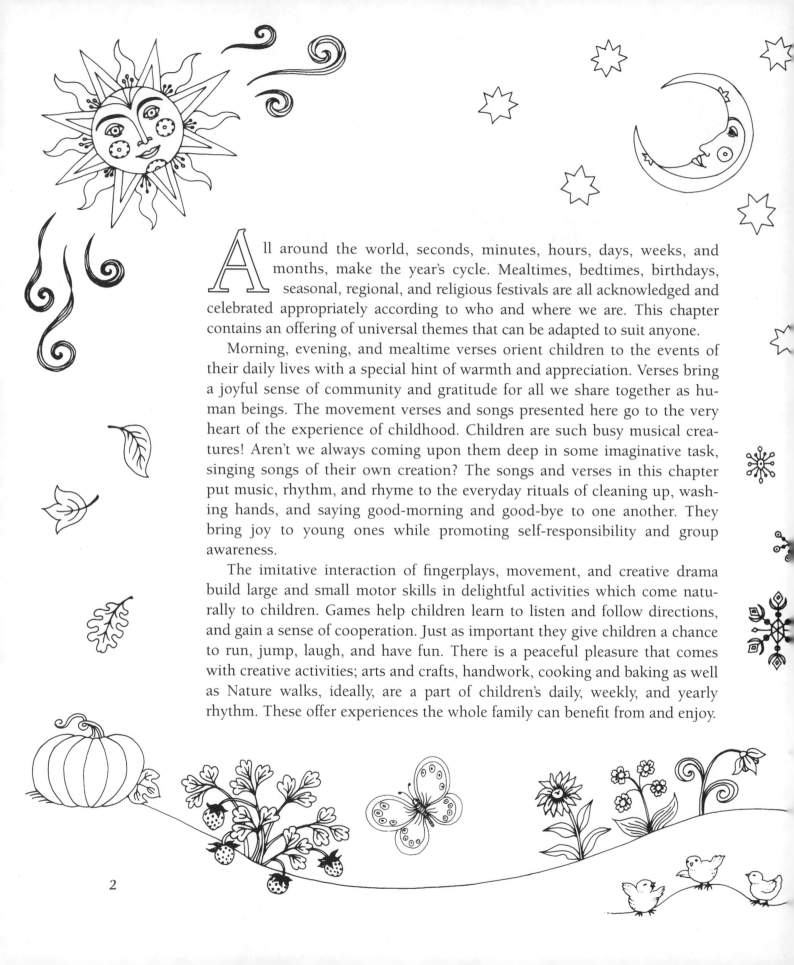

All around the world, seconds, minutes, hours, days, weeks, and months, make the year's cycle. Mealtimes, bedtimes, birthdays, seasonal, regional, and religious festivals are all acknowledged and celebrated appropriately according to who and where we are. This chapter contains an offering of universal themes that can be adapted to suit anyone.

Morning, evening, and mealtime verses orient children to the events of their daily lives with a special hint of warmth and appreciation. Verses bring a joyful sense of community and gratitude for all we share together as human beings. The movement verses and songs presented here go to the very heart of the experience of childhood. Children are such busy musical creatures! Aren't we always coming upon them deep in some imaginative task, singing songs of their own creation? The songs and verses in this chapter put music, rhythm, and rhyme to the everyday rituals of cleaning up, washing hands, and saying good-morning and good-bye to one another. They bring joy to young ones while promoting self-responsibility and group awareness.

The imitative interaction of fingerplays, movement, and creative drama build large and small motor skills in delightful activities which come naturally to children. Games help children learn to listen and follow directions, and gain a sense of cooperation. Just as important they give children a chance to run, jump, laugh, and have fun. There is a peaceful pleasure that comes with creative activities; arts and crafts, handwork, cooking and baking as well as Nature walks, ideally, are a part of children's daily, weekly, and yearly rhythm. These offer experiences the whole family can benefit from and enjoy.

All Year Round Verses and Poems

Winter, Spring, Summer, Autumn

Winter is white, springtime is green,
Summer is golden and autumn aflame,
Four lovely seasons to have in a year,
Sing them by color, sing them by name.

Four Seasons

Spring is showery, flowery, bowery.
Summer: hoppy, choppy, poppy.
Autumn: wheezy, sneezy, breezy.
Winter: slippy, drippy, nippy.

The Weather

Whether the weather be fine
Or whether the weather be not,
Whether the weather be cold
Or whether the weather be hot,
We'll weather the weather
Whatever the weather,
Whether we like it or not.

In the Garden — Seasons and Festivals

Margret Meyerkort, words ∼ Peter Patterson, music

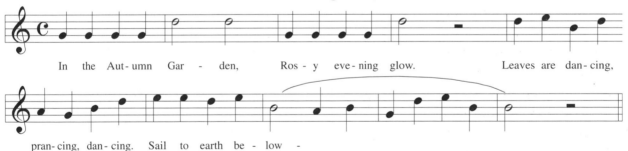

In the Aut-umn Gar-den, Ros-y eve-ning glow. Leaves are dan-cing, pran-cing, dan-cing. Sail to earth be-low -

1) In the winter garden,
   Seeds live warm below.
   Flowers waiting, waiting, waiting,
   For the spring to show…
2) In the springtime garden,
   Rosy morning glow.
   Sunshine falling, calling, falling,
   Seeds are waking so…

3) In the summer garden,
   Where we singing go.
   Light is flowing, glowing, flowing,
   White the roses grow.
   White the roses grow.

The Months

Sara Coleridge

January brings the snow,
Makes our feet and fingers glow.
February brings the rain,
Thaws the frozen lake again.
March brings breezes loud and shrill,
Stirs the dancing daffodil.
April brings the primrose sweet,
Scatters daisies at our feet.
May brings flocks of pretty lambs,
Skipping by their fleecy dams.
June brings tulips, lilies, roses,
Fills the children's hands with posies.

Hot July brings cooling showers,
Apricots and gillyflowers.
August brings the sheaves of corn,
Then the harvest home is borne.
Warm September brings the fruit,
And vegetables from stem to root.
Fresh October brings the pheasant,
Then to gather nuts is pleasant.
Dull November brings the blast,
Then the leaves are whirling fast.
Chill December brings the sleet,
Blazing fire, and Christmas treat.

Southern Hemisphere Months

Betty Jones

January, the sun shines bright,
The stars twinkle into the night.
February, so warm aglow,
While summer breezes begin to blow.
March comes marching merrily
Over land and over sea.
April showers begin to stir
The plants and animals, the waters pure.
May will start to bring the cold,
From the South Pole Winter bold.
June brings rain and winds so strong,
Windy, rainy, all day long.

July looks out upon the earth,
Seeds below await new birth.
August turns the tide of weather,
It seems now to be getting better.
September springs alive with joy,
Making happy each girl and boy.
October likes to breathe and blow,
All the colored flowers grow.
November days will bring more sun,
While over fields the children run.
December laughs with warmth of heart,
Making way for New Year's start.

The Moon

Eliza Follen

Oh, look at the moon she's shining up there,
Oh, mother, she looks like a lamp in the air!
Last week she was smaller and shaped like
   a bow,
But now she's grown bigger and round as
   an "O."
Pretty moon, pretty moon, blow your shine
   on the door
And make all bright on my nursery floor,
You shine on my playthings and show me
   their place
And I love to look up at your pretty, bright face,
And there is a star close by you and maybe
That small twinkling star is your baby!

The Sun Says

Eileen Hutchins

The sun says, "I glow,"
The wind says, "I blow,"
The stream says, "I flow,"
The tree says, "I grow,"
And Man says, "I know."

Birthday Song

Anonymous, words and music

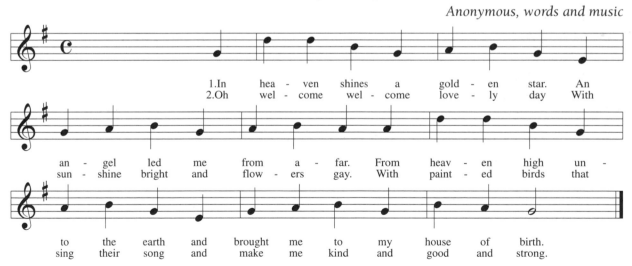

1.In hea - ven shines a gold - en star. An
2.Oh wel - come wel - come love - ly day With

an - gel led me from a - far. From heav - en high un -
sun - shine bright and flow - ers gay. With paint - ed birds that

to the earth and brought me to my house of birth.
sing their song and make me kind and good and strong.

Birthday Anticipation

When I have said my evening prayer
And my clothes are folded on the chair
And Mother switches off the light,
I'll still be ___ years old tonight.
But from the very break of day,
Before the children rise and play,
Before the darkness turns to gold,
Tomorrow I'll be ___ years old,
___ kisses when I wake,
___ candles on my cake.

This verse can be said at the end of the day with a birthday child. Fill in the blanks with the appropriate age of the child.

Mary's Birthday

Mary had a silver spoon,
Mary had a gay balloon,
Mary slept beneath the sun,
The day that she was one.

Mary had a golden bell,
Mary had a doll as well,
Mary had a bonnet blue,
The day that she was two.

Mary had a silken shawl,
Mary had a bouncing ball,
Mary threw the ball to me,
The day that she was three.

Mary had a Teddy Bear,
Mary had new shoes to wear,
Mary painted red her door,
The day that she was four.

Mary had a picture book,
Mary had a fishing hook,
Mary caught a fish alive,
The day that she was five.

Mary had a wooden train,
Mary had a horse's rein,
Mary built a house with sticks,
The day that she was six.

This is another verse of anticipation for a birthday. Use the birthday child's name instead of "Mary."

Number Verses

Eugene Schwartz, © 1993

One is the Sun that shines so bright,
One is the moon so high;
One is the day and one is the night,
One is the sheltering sky.
One is a head so still and tame,
Upon one body whole with health;
And *I* is the one and the special name
That only *I* can call myself!

Two are the eyes with which I see,
Two are the ears that hear;
Joy and sorrow both live in me,
And so do courage and fear.
Darkness and Light must together live,
Night and day are as sister and brother;
And two are the hands that receive and give,
To help myself or serve another.

Around me in the world I see
Beast and plant and stone.
Nature weaves her world as *Three*,
But I am three in one:
A head well-wrought for wisdom's work,
A heart hollowed by love;
Strong limbs to labor on the earth
As angels do above.

Summer and autumn, winter and spring,
Through *Four* seasons passes the year;
Fire and air, water and earth—
Out of these four does our whole world
    appear.

Five are the fingers upon each hand,
Each foot has its five toes;
Five rays has the star shining o'er the land,
Five petals has the rose.
And when with limbs outstretched I alight,
Like a five-pointed star
All the world I make bright!

The Snow Queen casts *Six*-pointed flakes
On stormy winds to ride;
The crystal with its six clear walls
In deepest earth abides;
When the busy bee builds honeycombs
He sculpts them with six sides.
Wherever Light would find a home,
In storm, or cave, or honeycomb,
Six is its chosen number and form.

Alphabet Verses

A: We say "Ah" to the wonderful things that are,
The rainbow arch and the watching star.
When day departs, a single star,
Marks how bright the heavens are.
See afar the moon embark,
Upon the ocean of the dark.

B: Blow, breezes, blow! Flow, rivers, flow!
Shine, sun, shine! And grow, flowers, grow!
The bears who look for berries early,
Find bigger, better berries, surely.
But bees must wait til buds are open,
Before they buzz along the blossoms.

C: C is cutting and clear and bold,
Crystal and icy, crackily and cold.

D: D is a deed to be done for men,
Dangerous dragon to dare in his den.
Deep in the earth, when days are darkest,
Dwells the summer's dawn.

E: I see, I feel, I gladly greet,
The earth beneath my eager feet.

F: The farmer flings the fruitful seed,
Afar from the furrowed field.
Fast, the foaming feathers fly!

G: Go you grim and grisly bear,
Growling in your gloomy lair!
Gleeful goblins gathering glittering gold,
Growl the gale in gloomy glen.

H: Hey, ho! The happy hunter's horn,
High over hill and hedge and thorn.
Hurling helpers heave high!

I: The light that shines in heaven high,
Likes to weave the colors bright,
Sheds his kindness from the sky,
Gives us right and strength and light.
A little of his light am I,
A candle in the night.

J: Jolly Jack and joyful Jill,
Jumping down the jaggy hill.

K: K is King, so keen and kind,
Keeping the kingdom for all mankind.

L: Lovely colors gleaming brightly,
Laughing waters, lapping lightly.
Light that lingers, long and low,
Makes the lovely colors glow.

M: Musing mid the moonbeams mild,
Mindful moved the marveling child.

N: Now the night is nigh, it's noon,
Nimble gnomes beneath the moon.

O: Alone upon the throne of gold,
With rope of purple, fold on fold,
The Monarch Lord of lands untold,
Ruled his folk in days of old.

P: Peerless Princess, proudly dancing,
Tulips tall and peacocks prancing.

Q: Queen quite quiet by the river,
Watch the quail, shiver, quiver.

R: Rustle of trees and ripples of rain,
Roaring rivers across the plain.

S: Sailing ships on swelling seas,
Shining sun and summer breeze.
Snow and ice and silvered hedges,
Sleet and slush and slides and sledges.
See summer, shall the shining sun,
Surely bless the slender shoots.

T: Tempest taught the tender tree.

U: Under umbrellas until the rain
subsides.

V: Very valiant soldiers invade
Various lands for victory.

W: Watchful, we will walk together,
Wander wide in windy weather.

X: Cunning, crafty fox

Y: Yesterday the young monkey yelled
And yodeled and jumped all around.

Z: Zing, zing, zoom, the zither is playing
a tune;
It plays so sweet and far away,
Zing, zing, zoom.

Cleaning Up

Wendalyn von Meyenfeldt

In a little mousie hole,
There lived a little mousie,
Who wore a checkered apron
And kept a tidy housie.
With her wee small broom,
She swept and swept her room,
And every little shelf,
She tidied by herself.

She put her babies in bed,
Then fairy stories she read.
She was a good, kind mousie,
She kept a tidy housie.

*Act out verse with a finger puppet mouse
before clean-up time.*

It's Time

Betty Jones

Tick-tock, goes the clock
What does it have to say?
It's time now to clean up our room
And put our toys away.
Tick-tock, let's clean up
It's story-time today.
Dollies, trollies, all our treasures
Put them gently now away.

*One child can tick-tock with rhythm sticks and
pass them to other children to maintain the beat
of cleaning-up time! Replace "story-time" with
"circle-time," "outdoor- or garden-time," etc. to
mark transitions from one activity to another.*

Shimmering Sea

Betty Jones

A verse for washing hands before a meal.

Flip and dip my hands like fish
In the silver sea,
Fly and dry them in the air
And sit me down to tea.

*An essential oil is nice to add to the water or
put a drop on the child's hands after washing.*

Move hands through water like fish.

Flick hands to dry.

Blessings on the Meal

Betty Jones

Begin by holding hands at the table.

Thanks to the Earth,
Thanks to the Sun,
Thanks to the Rain
For all they have done
To bring me my food

So strong I will grow,
And loving in life
From my heart I will show:
"Blessings on the meal."

Shake hands with neighbors in unison.

Mealtime Blessing Songs

Christian Morganstern, words ∽ P. Bauman, music

Earth who gives to us our food. Sun who makes it ripe and good.

Dear - est Earth and Dear - est Sun. Joy a - nd love for all you have do - ne.

Joy a - nd love for all you have do - o - o - ne.

Anonymous, words ∽ Margret Meyerkort, music

Bless - ing on the blo - o - ssom. Bless - ing on the

root. Bless - ing on the leaf and stem.

Bless - ing on the fruit.

Goodbye Song

Anonymous, words and music

Good bye now, good bye now, we leave you now and home we go. Good

bye now, good bye now. Good bye to all of you. It's

time to go or we'll be late. Let (Mar - tin) lead us to the gate. Good

bye now, good bye now, we'll see you soon a - gain.

Replace "Martin" with name of child who leads the goodbye.

Bedtime

Thomas Hood

The evening is coming, the sun sinks to rest,
The rooks are all flying straight to the nest,
"Caw!" says the rook, as he flies overhead;
"It's time little people were going to bed!"
The flowers are closing; the daisy's asleep;
The primrose is buried in slumber so deep.
Shut up for the night is the pimpernel red,
It's time little people were going to bed.
"Goodnight, little people, goodnight, and
    goodnight,
Sweet dreams to your eyelids 'til dawning
    of light,

The evening has come, there's no more
    to be said,
It's time little people were going to bed!"
The butterfly drowsy, has folded its wing,
The bees are returning, no more the
    birds sing,
Their labor is over, their nestlings are fed;
It's time little people were going to bed!
Here comes the pony, his work is all done,
Down through the meadow he takes a
    good run,
Up go his heels and down goes his head,
It's time little people were going to bed!

All Year Round
Movement and Creative Drama

Young children are growing into their bodies, and they are learning to coordinate their movements in activities that help develop their muscles and organs. All the gestures and movements they are exposed to are experienced deeply and imitated outwardly in their encounters with the people and the world around them. Thus, it is helpful for the adults in a young child's life to be aware that the adult's body language teaches the child. It is a wonderful aid to a child's development for parents and teachers to move and gesture with care and consciousness when in the child's presence. As children gain skill and mastery over their bodies, they coordinate their movements in imaginative activity. A child may become a leaf, a fairy, or an animal. These movements are reflections of their deep feelings and experiences of imagination.

Keeping to the rhythm of the verses helps hold the children in the flow of movements, which may occur in a circle, moving in place, forward, backward, up, down, or turning. As much as possible, allow the children to improvise, testing their coordination and physical limits safely. Young children's skill and ability levels vary greatly. Tailor games and dramatizations to suit the group so that no one is left out. It is fine to have more than one child acting out a character or characters at the same time. This helps them avoid self-consciousness and relieves inhibitions. The important thing for the adult to remember is to move consciously with slow and certain purpose. Enjoy the creative expression of movement, drama, and games as personal and social activities.

Morning Song

Anonymous, words and music

Good morn-ing dear earth. Good morn-ing dear sun. Good morn-ing dear

rocks and the flow-ers eve-ry one. Good morn-ing dear beasts. And the

birds in the trees. Good morn-ing to you and good morn-ing to me.

1st line: Children crouch, touching the floor.

2nd line: Rise, extending arms to sky.

3rd line: Crouch; knock fists on floor at "rocks."

4th line: Remain crouching; wiggle fingers and sway hands at "flowers."

5th line: Remain crouching; put hands on head like horns at "beasts."

6th line: Flap arms like wings while rising to stand.

7th line: Straighten arms; bow at the waist at "you."

8th line: Stand upright; cross arms over heart.

End by extending hands to one another and shake in unison while saying, "good morning, good morning."

Morning

Begin by standing in a circle.

The earth is firm beneath my feet,

The sun shines bright above,

And here stand I, so straight and strong,

All things to know and love.

Good morning, good morning!

Squat and touch ground.

Stand and raise arms above.

Cross arms over chest.

Spread arms outward to sides.

Shake hands with neighbors in unison.

Morning Verse

Begin by standing in a circle.

Down is the earth,	*Touch the ground.*
Up is the sky,	*Rise with arms above.*
There are my friends	*Gesture outward.*
And here am I.	*Cross arms over chest.*
Good morning, good morning.	*Shake hands with neighbors in unison.*

Goodbye

Begin by holding hands in a circle.

Merry have we met	*Walk in rhythm toward center.*
And merry have we been,	*Walk in rhythm to periphery.*
Merry shall we part	*Let go of hands, turn around in place one time,*
And merry meet again.	*then walk toward center.*
"Goodbye, goodbye."	*Shake hands in unison.*

Early Morning
Hilare Belloc

*Begin by standing in a circle with arms
crossed over chest.*

The moon on the one hand,	*Hold left arm out to the side.*
The sun on the other,	*Hold right arm out to the side.*
The moon is my sister,	*Cross left arm over chest.*
The sun is my brother,	*Cross right arm over chest.*
The moon at my left,	*Stretch left arm up at side.*
The sun at my right,	*Stretch right arm up at side.*
My brother good morning,	*Lower left arm down at side.*
My sister good night.	*Lower right arm down at side.*
Goodbye, Goodbye!	*Shake hands with neighbor in rhythm.*

I Have
Betty Jones

Begin by sitting in a circle.

Eyes to look,	*Look all around.*
Read a book.	*Read imaginary book.*
Ears to hear,	*Cup hand to ear.*
Far and near.	*Bend at waist backward, then forward.*
Nose to smell,	*Inhale through nose.*
Very well.	*Exhale through nose.*
Teeth to bite,	*Chomp teeth.*
Chew just right.	*Chew with teeth.*
Feet to walk,	*Stomp feet.*
Block after block.	*Continue stomping.*
Arms to fold,	*Fold arms over chest.*
Lots to hold.	*Stretch arms forward.*
Hands to try,	*Hold out hands, palms up.*
Wave good-bye!	*Wave hand.*

Can You?
Betty Jones

Reach for the ceiling, touch the ground,
Tap your fingers without a sound,
Stand up again, turn 'round in place,
Bend your knees and tap your face,
Hop up now, clap 1-2-3,
Sit down now, quiet as can be.

Standing in a circle, act out as indicated.

Do You?
Betty Jones

Do you feel joyful? Do you feel proud?
All who do clap your hands out loud!
Do you feel joyful? Do you feel proud?
All who do snap your fingers out loud!
Do you feel joyful? Do you feel proud?
All who do stomp your feet out loud!
Do you feel joyful? Do you feel proud?
All who do jump up and down out loud!

Children walk joyfully and proudly around a
circle, stopping to perform indicated movements.
Invite children to invent their own movements.

Movement Game

Can you walk on two legs, two legs, two legs?	*Walk clockwise around a circle.*
Can you walk on two legs round and round and round?	*Continue walking.*
I can walk on two legs, two legs, two legs,	*Turn and walk counterclockwise.*
I can walk on two legs round and round and round!	*Continue walking.*
Can you hop on one leg, one leg, one leg?	*Hop clockwise around circle.*
Can you hop on one leg round and round and round?	*Continue hopping.*
I can hop on one leg, one leg, one leg,	*Turn and hop counterclockwise.*
I can hop on one leg round and round and round!	*Continue hopping.*

Continue making new verses with corresponding movements, like jump on two legs, wave with one hand, clap with two hands, etc.

If

Begin by standing in a circle.

If I were a little bird high up in the sky,	
This is how I'd flap my wings and fly, fly, fly.	*Flap arms up and down.*
If I were a friendly dog going for a run,	
This is how I'd wag my tail when having fun.	*"Wag" behind.*
If I were a cat, I'd sit by the fireplace	*Kneel.*
And this is how I'd use my paws to wash my face.	*Use sides of hands as paws to "wash face."*
If I were a rabbit small, in the woods I'd roam,	
This is how I'd dig and burrow for my home.	*Kneel; cup hands and make digging gestures.*
If I were an elephant big and strong,	
This is how I'd have my trunk and walk along.	*Stand; clasp hands together with arms straight down, swing arms while walking in a circle.*
If I were a kangaroo I would leap and bound,	
This is how I'd rock from side to side.	*Leap forward, then back; lean side to side.*
If I were a tall giraffe living in the zoo,	
This is how I'd bend my neck and look at you.	*Bend far forward and look all around.*

The Elephant

Begin by standing in a circle.

An elephant goes like this and that,
He's terribly big
And terribly fat.
He has no fingers,
He has no toes,
But goodness, gracious,
What a nose!

Rock from side to side.
Stretch entire body.
Stretch arms out wide.
Wiggle fingers.
Wiggle toes.
Bend body forward, clasp hands together with
*   arms straight down, and swing arms.*

Leap, Slide, Dip, and Glide

Betty Jones

Frogs jump and leap,
Chicks hop and peep,
Snakes slip and slide,
Mice squeak and hide,
Dolphins swim and flip,
Seagulls glide and dip,
Horses trot clip-clop,
Bunnies bounce hippity-hop,
And what about me?
I _____ high as I can, see?!
And now sit quiet as can be.

In a circle, children imitate movement and sounds
of creatures identified. Blank line invites their own
movement, e.g., skip, jump, hop on one foot, walk,
etc., which is imitated by everyone in circle.

Visit to a Farm

I went to visit a farm one day,
I saw a cow across the way,
And what do you think I heard it say?
MOO-MOO-MOO!

Repeat the verse, inserting different farm
animals and imitating their voices.

Turn Around

Betty Jones

As I was walking one fine day
I turned to look the other way
When I heard a wee voice say:
(whisper) Come follow me. . .

Turning round to just see where
Who could be a-speaking there,
I saw a light so bright and fair:
(whisper) Come follow me. . .

On tip-toe now, turning round,
I sought the light without a sound
Until I reached the fairy mound:
(whisper) Come follow me. . .

Here I turned around in place
The fairies are too bright to face,
So with a skip and a hop back home I race:
(whisper) Come follow me. . .

*Begin by walking in one direction around a circle.
All stop, make a half turn, "look," and take a few
steps in new direction until the words "Come follow
me." Turn halfway around again, then step in
rhythm until "Come follow me." Then at "tip-toe"
make a quarter turn and tip-toe to center of circle
until "Come follow me." Then all turn to face out
toward periphery, skip and hop back to place, and
end by sitting down on the ground.*

Go, My Pony, Go

Go, my pony, go,
King sun begins to glow,
We're riding into spring,
Ring, oh bluebell, ring!

Trot, my pony, trot,
The sun grows big and hot,
We're riding into summer's day,
All wreathed with roses, red and gay!

Gallop, pony, gallop on,
Hey dee hop, the summer is gone,
We're riding into autumn now,
The leaves are falling from the bough.

Stop, my pony, whoa!
The cold brings frost and snow,
Winter's not the time to ride,
The roads are icy far and wide.

Rest, my pony, rest,
Sleep now in your nest,
We're dreaming into Heaven far,
And flying swift from star to star.

*Children trot like ponies in a circle following
the pace indicated at each season.*

All Year Round
Fingerplays and Riddles

Fingerplays and brain-teasing riddles help children build their fine motor co-ordination with the aid of their imagination. The child translates the spoken words into finger movements. As with other fine motor activities, fingerplays can be challenging, and it is only through joyful practice that all five fingers will actually strengthen and gain dexterity.

Riddles require concentration, as does the effort to register verbal clues and fit them together to solve a riddle. Children can learn to make up their own riddles by describing something without naming it, gradually building their verbal skills and sharpening their wits. Then you better be on your toes! How fortunate that these fingerplays and riddles are so much fun!

Ten Fingers

I have ten little fingers	*Stretch hands out in front.*
And they belong to me,	*Point to self.*
I can make them do things,	*Rub hands together.*
Would you like to see?	*Open hands, palms up.*
I can shut them up tight,	*Make fists.*
Or I can make them wide,	*Extend fingers.*
I can put them together,	*Clasp hands.*
Or make them all hide,	*Put hands behind back.*
I can make them jump high,	*Raise hands overhead.*
I can make them jump low,	*Place hands on floor.*
I can fold them quietly,	*Fold hands together.*
And hold them just so.	

My Hands

Upon my head my hands I place,
On my shoulders, on my face,
On my waist, at my side,
Now behind me they will hide,
Now I'll stretch them way up high,
Make my fingers swiftly fly,
I'll hold them up in front of me,
And quickly clap them, one, two, three!

Begin standing in a circle and act out as indicated.

Through the Year

Betty Jones

*Use these fingerplays in their specific season
or all together anytime.*

In autumn time the leaves will fall   *Cup hands at mouth to call "o-o-o-h-h."*
As Brother Wind blows his call,   *Twirl and dance fingers around.*
Twirling, whirling, dancing 'round   *Turn palms upward and flutter fingers.*
Leaves of scarlet, gold, and brown.

Winter comes with ice and snow   *Flutter fingers downward from overhead.*
Covers o'er the seeds below,   *Spread hands over floor in covering gesture.*
Stark the trees and cold the air,   *Shiver and hug self.*
King Winter rules the land, beware!   *Fold arms over chest and stand regally.*

Spring is here and birdies sing,   *Pinch index finger and thumb open and closed.*
Flower Fairies dance in a ring,   *Stretch arms in front of body and flutter fingers.*
The sun shines bright, the children play   *Lift hands above head; flutter fingers.*
Happy, humming each spring day!   *Sway body from side to side; flutter fingers.*

Crystal waters, warmth of sun,   *Hold hands high, palms up; lower arms to waist.*
Golden sand, oh, what fun!   *Turn palms down; flutter fingers; clasp hands.*
Seaside treasures, waves of foam,   *Roll hands over each other.*
Summer breezes, blow me home!   *Flutter fingers at mouth; blow them away.*

Two Little Blackbirds

Two little blackbirds, sitting on a wall,   *Begin with hands closed, thumbs up.*
One named Peter, one named Paul,   *Wiggle one thumb, then the other.*
Fly away Peter, fly away Paul,   *Hide one thumb around back, then the other.*
Come back Peter, come back Paul.   *Return hands, one at a time, with thumbs up.*

Air

Look up, look down, look all around,
Look everywhere.
You couldn't live without me,
I'm even in your chair—
What is my name?

Counting to Ten and Back Again

Betty Jones

One, two, cock-a-doodle-doo!
Cock-a-doodle-doo.
Three, four, horses that snore!
Honk-shnoo.
Five, six, chirping chicks!
Cheep, cheep.
Seven, eight, dogs bark at the gate!
Bow, wow.
Nine, ten, pigs oink in the pen!
Oink, oink.
Ten, nine, crows on a line!
Caw, caw.

Eight, seven, doves from heaven!
Roo, coo.
Six, five, fish leap and dive!
Splish, splash.
Four, three, laugh chimpanzees!
Hee, hee, hee.
Two, one, we're all done!

Clap hands together twice.
Present fingers as indicated, voice animal sounds, and drop fingers as indicated.

All Year Round Games

Tommy Tucker

OBJECT: To get back to the empty space first

PROCEDURE: Players stand in a circle holding hands. Tommy Tucker walks around the inside of the circle. She puts her right hand between two players and says, "Tommy Tucker, run for your supper!" The rule is that the two players cannot start running until the word "supper." The two players run in opposite directions around the circle and the one who gets back first is the new Tommy Tucker. Repeat. In addition to "run," Tommy Tucker may also command that children walk, skip, hop, gallop, slide, tip-toe, etc.

Surprise Jar

MATERIALS: Jar, slips of paper with easy-to-read or simply drawn messages

METHOD: Each child takes a slip of paper from the jar and must do what the note describes.

IDEAS: Acting out chick bursting forth from egg, wiggly worm, special cleaning tasks, physical exercises, toy choices, etc.

Phone Fun

MATERIALS: Soup cans attached to either end of a long string

METHOD: Let the children show how they answer the phone. Guide the activity by encouraging them to use words such as "Hello?" "Who's calling?" "Just a moment, please," emergency phone numbers, directions to come to a friend's house, etc.

Odd and Even Game

Eugene Schwartz, © 1993

The children form two lines; one line wears crowns bearing odd numbers, the other wears crowns with even numbers.

LINE ONE:
We are the Odd Numbers,
Oh, so lonely!
We haven't any friends
By night or day;
Ah, for one friend,
One friend only,
To hop and skip and run and play!

LINE TWO:
Here we come,
The Even Numbers!
We're your friends,
We'll stand by you;
Call our names and we'll come romping,
Dancing, stomping, two by two!

Calling out their numbers in turn, the children pair up, take hands, and skip together to music played by their teacher.

All Year Round
Art and Handwork

Coloring

This activity gives children the opportunity to be expressive in color and form. The parent or teacher need to do nothing more than encourage them to fill the page and to produce shading strokes. Coloring paper should be large enough to allow free, sweeping strokes. Adults can remove the paper from chubby crayons and break them into 1½-inch lengths so young ones can draw with the broad side of the crayon, allowing them to experience the layering and blending of colors. Beeswax block crayons also work well for this. A verse said together before this activity sets the mood for a colorful journey:

Coloring Verse

Wendalyn von Meyenfeldt

There is a golden castle,
As golden as the day,
But only with our crayons
Can we find the way, for,
Red is the King,
Blue is the Queen,
Snow White their baby,
The Hunter is green,
Purple the mountains
Where the Seven Dwarfs dwell,
Orange-gold the treasure,
They dig and delve.

Colorful Journeying

Betty Jones

With my crayons I will go,
Journeying o'er the bright rainbow,
Red and yellow, green and blue,
Orange and purple, that will do,
Now let's see where they take me to.

Children sit at tables with hands folded until basket comes and colors are selected.

Watercolor Painting

It is truly beautiful to watch children marvel as the creative power of color is experienced in the blending and flowing of primary colors. Watercolor painting provides a color experience free from any proposed imagery. Allow the children to spontaneously experience their own creativity.

Children delight in being Rainbow Fairy Helpers who assist in preparing for watercolor painting. You will need wide, tapered watercolor brushes with long, thick wooden handles; good-quality watercolor paper precut to at least 11 x 15 inches; quality watercolors in tubes; baby food or other small jars; large wide-mouthed jars; clean sponges; soft cotton rags; painting smocks (old shirts with sleeves cut down); a rectangular basin or sink with stopper; and a 15-x-20-inch Masonite board.

Begin by filling large jars with water. Next fill the rectangular basin with water and put the watercolor paper in to soak. While paper is soaking, put a squeeze of watercolor paint in the bottom of each small jar. Initially use only red, yellow, and blue. Add about an inch of water to each small jar. The children can stir the paint with their brushes, but they must be shown and told how to always rinse the brush in water and wipe it on their painting cloths before putting it in another color. When they have finished mixing their paint and wiping their brushes, they may pour out their rinse water and get a fresh jar. Each carries their water to the painting table. Give each child a sponge to wet and wipe their painting board in preparation for the paper. The adult carefully places the soaked paper on the board and gently sponges the paper flat, removing air bubbles and creases that form underneath.

At the beginning of each watercolor session, an adult demonstrates for the child to imitate the proper way to hold and use the brush. The brush should rest between the thumb and index finger and is grasped gently around its silver collar, allowing easy manipulation in dipping and painting. Dip the brush carefully into the paint, then gently stroke the paint onto the wet paper. Let the different colors "meet, dance, and speak" with one another. Model cleaning the brush thoroughly before choosing a new color.

Vary each painting session by concentrating on the "conversation" between two primary colors before graduating to the three primary colors in subsequent sessions. When the children have finished painting, they clean their spaces and equipment, and the adult safely stows their paintings to dry (preferably *on* the painting board).

Before passing out the fairy wands (paint brushes), set the special mood before each painting session by saying a verse together.

Rainbow Fairy Ring

Betty Jones

Rainbow Fairies sing	*Raise arms outward, then overhead; fingertips meet to form a ring.*
In my Rainbow Fairy Ring.	*Hold ring gesture.*
The colors that you bring	*Flutter fingers outward; lower ring over paper.*
Together they will sing	*Hold fluttering ring gesture.*
In my Rainbow Fairy Ring!	*Bring fingertips together as they stop fluttering, hold ring gesture over paper.*
	Then children are free to spread their rainbow light!

Handwork

These activities foster in children respect for what their hands can create and for the materials they use. They gain appreciation for the harmony of color, form, function, and beauty that fills their lives. Manipulating the materials and tools helps children develop fine motor skills and coordination. As they learn to follow instructions, children build sensibility for their body geography, learning left, right, forward, backward, up, down, in, and out.

In fiber arts activities, natural materials are recommended, such as 100% cotton yardage, batting, and embroidery thread, and 100% wool fleece, felt, and thick-gauged yarn. It is also helpful to supply the children with large-eyed needles. Make children aware that their efforts transform raw materials into useful articles or fanciful gifts. Encouraging children to be thrifty with their materials makes them sensitive to the existence of limited resources.

Appropriate verses and rhymes said together before the handwork or craft sessions prepare children for the activities by helping them imagine themselves engaged in the upcoming tasks. They present imaginative pictures that the children can relate to more readily than to instructions alone. Encourage little ones to tell their own stories during these activities, a lively way to inspire their creativity.

The Little Men (Handwork Verse)

Oh! Where are the merry, merry little men
To join us in our play?
And where are the busy, busy little men
To help us work today?
Upon each hand a little band
For work or play is ready.
The first to come
Is Master Thumb;
Then Pointer, strong and steady;
Then Tall Man high;

And just close by
The Feeble Man doth linger;
And last of all, so fair and small,
The baby—Little Finger.
Yes! Here are the merry, merry little men,
To join us in our play;
And here are the busy, busy little men,
To help us work today.

My Two Hands

Betty Jones

I have two hands
And fingers ten,
I am the King
And they are my men.
When my teacher shows me
The work that I must do,
The King can surely go
And all of his men, too!

Hold up both hands.
Wiggle fingers of both hands.
Point with thumb to self.
Wiggle fingers.
Replace with "mother" or "father."
Hold hands out to adult.
Cross arms over chest.
Hold hands out to adult to receive
  handwork materials.

Knot-Tying

Betty Jones

Knotting is easy, it's kind of teasy.
You start by taking each end,
Then cross one over and send it through.
Pull it tightly, that will do!
One more time the other way,
Now you have a knot, okay?

Practice with shoelaces that are wide
and easy to handle.

Bow-Tying

Betty Jones

How to make a bow I know!
Take each end and make a bridge,
Cross one over and under the other.
Once each is on the other side
They can wave and say, "Hi Brother!"
Next to their Sister, Loop-de-loo,
Round about, under and all the way
    through.
Pull so carefully, as you know,
Each Loop-de-loo makes a lovely bow!

Cross laces one over the other.
Pull one lace over and under other.

Lace ends wave in crossed position.
Make loop with one lace.
Other lace goes round and under first loop
    to form a second loop.
Pull this second loop through carefully.
Secure bow with a firm tug on both loops.

Finger Crochet

MATERIALS: Thick wool yarn when first learning; any wool yarn or cotton string once mastered

PROCEDURE: Make a slip knot. Maintaining the loop of the slip knot, use two fingers to pull another loop through, while holding on to the tail and not letting the loop get too large. Give tail a little tug. Continue to make loops until desired length. Add different colors as desired by knotting two yarns together. The lengths can then be wound and lightly stitched into a spiral to be used as a doll's rug or as a pot holder or mat. Three long lengths can be braided together and knotted at ends to make a jump rope. Let your imagination fly!

Finger Crochet Verse

Use your little pinchers,
Go into the cave.
Grab the little snake,
My, but you're brave!
Pull it back through,
So two of you can play.
Close up the hole,
So he can't get away!

Making Knitting Needles

MATERIALS: ¼-inch wooden doweling, or any size comparable to standard knitting needle size; coarse and fine sandpaper; 2 large beads

PROCEDURE: Cut two pieces of doweling to 12 inches long. Using the coarse sandpaper, sand a balanced taper. Finish with the fine sandpaper. Glue a bead to the flat end.

Learning to Knit Verse

Joan Marcus

In through the front door,
Running round the back,
Looking through the window,
Off comes Jack!

First Knitting Project

MATERIALS: Size 4 or 5 needles; worsted wool yarn

PROCEDURE: Cast on 15 stitches loosely. Knit 1 row. Slip 1 stitch; knit to end. Repeat last row for 5½ inches. Cast off. This simple shape can become a doll's bed, a canoe, or…?

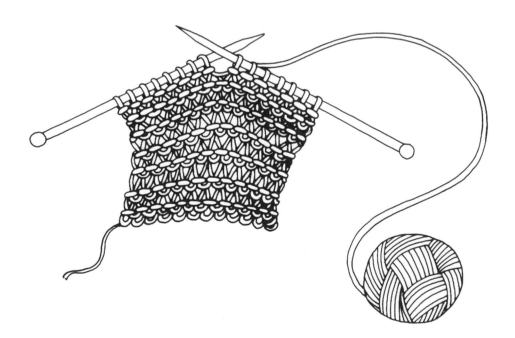

Yarn Dolls

MATERIALS: Wool yarn of various colors, cardboard, scissors

PROCEDURE: Cut the cardboard in rectangles, the body (which includes the head) being longer than the arms. Give the children wool of their color choice and have them wind neatly around the cardboard lengthwise until the desired thickness. Tie at the top edge of the body and cut wool at the bottom edge to take out the cardboard. Tie at neck to form head. Tie at each end of arms and take out cardboard. Tie at either wrist for hands. Slip arms up under neck and tie securely. Tie at the waist and leave the rest of the body to hang as a skirt, or divide wool evenly and tie at ankles to create legs and feet.

Modeling with Beeswax

Beeswax is a warm and wonderful medium. Modeling beeswax can be purchased from one of the suppliers on the Resource List at the back of the book. It is very pliable and warming to the hands and has a delicious honey scent that seems to stimulate the tactile, visual, and olfactory senses.

Begin the activity with a fingerplay preparing little hands to receive their beeswax.

Bees-Waxing

Betty Jones

Zooma-zooma-zee.	*Flutter fingers and wave hands from side to side.*
Busy little bee!	*Make circles in air with fluttering fingers.*
Wax you've made for me.	*Cup hands together, fingertips touching.*
What I'll make we'll see.	*Bring cupped hands to face, peek inside.*
Zooma-zooma-zee.	*Flutter fingers and wave hands from side to side.*

Children will love listening to a nature or seasonal story while they sit in a circle, warming the small ball of colored wax they've taken from the basket. This will spark the imagination and give them time to warm and soften their beeswax.

Play Dough

1 cup flour
½ cup salt
1 cup water

1 tablespoon vegetable oil
2 teaspoons cream of tartar

Mix all ingredients well to remove lumps. Cook on stove, stirring constantly, until consistency changes. It should be too thick to stir, but it should have a sheen. Knead to cool, but it may be handed to children while still a little warm. Makes enough for 2 or 3 children.

All Year Round Cooking and Baking

This activity will bring the children much enjoyment while also teaching them rules of hygiene, measurement, and skill in utilizing kitchen tools. High-quality, wholesome ingredients should be used in cooking and baking. Ideally, a small garden plot from which to pick fresh vegetables, fruits, and herbs gives children the immediate experience of tending the earth and growing the foods that are as dependent on the seasonal cycles of time as the children are themselves. A mood of appreciation and anticipation makes the harvest even more delightful. Here is a verse to share before this social activity (after all hands have been washed!):

Verse for Cooking and Baking
Betty Jones

Bless the food that I now take,
Bless my hands that I may make
Something good to cook or bake.

Simple Whole Wheat Bread Loaf or Buns

1 teaspoon plus 2 tablespoons
   honey
1 tablespoon active dry yeast
3 cups warm water

2 tablespoons oil
1 tablespoon sea salt
8½ to 9½ cups
   whole wheat flour

Please note: this recipe can easily be doubled, tripled, or even quadrupled if you are working with many children. As is, the bun option in this recipe serves the kneading needs of six to eight children.

In a large mixing bowl, dissolve 1 teaspoon honey and the yeast in ½ cup warm water (105° F to 115° F); let soak about 10 minutes. Mix remaining water with 2 tablespoons honey, oil, and salt, then add to yeast mixture. Add flour gradually and mix well until dough comes away from sides of bowl easily, then remove to a floured board and let sit about 10 minutes. Knead for 10 to 15 minutes, adding enough flour to make a smooth, elastic, nonsticky dough. (Exact quantity of flour will vary each time.) Place dough in oiled bowl, cover with a damp cloth, and let rise in a warm place until just doubled in bulk (about 2 hours). Punch dough down; knead for a few minutes. (Children love to give the dough that first punch!)

If you are working with several children, divide the dough into large bun-size pieces and pass it out to them. Have the children knead and work their dough on a floured surface for 5 to 10 minutes. Encourage a final "bun" shape (not flat); inscribe the child's initials on the top of their bun with a fork. Bake buns for 15 to 20 minutes.

If you do not intend to make buns, shape punched-down dough into loaves. Place loaves in oiled bread pans (about 9 x 5 x 3 inches) and let rise again until nearly double in bulk. Preheat oven to 350° F. Bake about 45 minutes, or until crust is a nice golden brown. Remove from pan immediately and cool. For a nice crust, brush top with oil while still hot.

Quick Bread

1 cup molasses, or 3/4 cup molasses
   plus 1/4 cup honey
2 cups buttermilk or yogurt
2 tablespoons soda
3 3/4 cups whole wheat flour

1/4 cup wheat germ
1/2 teaspoon salt
1/2 cup raisins
1/2 cup mixed, crushed nuts

In a small bowl, mix the wet ingredients together. In a large bowl, combine the dry ingredients. Add the wet to the dry ingredients and mix well. Bake in preheated 375° F oven for 40 minutes in a greased and floured oblong cake pan. Cool before slicing.

Irish Soda Bread

3 cups whole wheat flour
1 cup all-purpose flour
1 teaspoon salt
1 tablespoon baking soda

3/4 teaspoon baking powder
1 1/2 to 2 cups buttermilk
Raisins (optional)

Preheat oven to 375° F. Mix dry ingredients. Add milk to make a firm, soft dough. Knead dough on a floured board for 2 to 3 minutes, until smooth, mixing in raisins, if desired. Form into a round. For a traditional look, slash the top with a knife in a cross. Bake on a greased sheet at 375° F for 35 to 40 minutes.

A Child's Seasonal Treasury

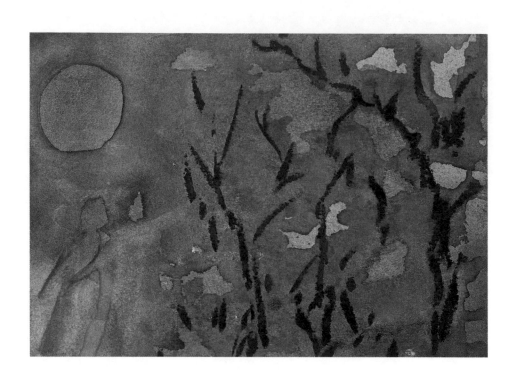

Autumn

Brother Wind howls, blowing the leaves from the trees. Father Sun's warmth and light are subsiding. The world appears to be slipping into the cold promise of winter, and all prepare for the darkness that enfolds the world. Yet inside each of us sparks the light and warmth of the human spirit. We kindle our light within as winter approaches.

Autumn is the time to celebrate the Spirits in festivals like Halloween (October 31), and Dia de los Muertos (Day of the Dead, November 1). It is a time to celebrate festivals of the light conquering the darkness, as in Michaelmas. It is a time when families can create their own light festivals and enjoy a lantern walk in the night.

Autumn is also harvest time, when the fruits of human labor are gathered and transformed by human hands. This is when we celebrate the bounty of the earth. Most cultures enjoy joyful harvest gatherings. In America the Thanksgiving feast celebrates this bounty, with friends and family gathering gratefully before the well-laid table.

The sights, sounds, smells, tastes, and feelings, both tactile and emotional, are the doors of learning for the young child. Thus, walks together out in Nature bring children the crackle of dead sticks underfoot, the musty smell of autumn leaves, and their glorious colors to live in the memory and imagination.

This chapter is full of verses, song, and activities celebrating the mood of harvest and the falling leaves. Look out! There are goblins about. There's lots of Halloween fun in verses, games, and song. Here is a bountiful offering of projects and recipes to enjoy with your children.

What do you remember from your own childhood that calls to heart and mind the beauty of this time of year? It is from this source of joy and sharing that the children in your care will be nourished and take in deeply the gifts of autumn-tide.

Autumn Verses and Poems

Sing and Do

Margret Meyerkort, words and music

S - i - ng, si - ng of the Har - vest Wreath bind - ing. S - i - ng,

si - ng of the Har - vestWreath mind - ing. Sing of the wheat and the

oats and the rye. Sing of the rib - bon to hang it up

high. S - i - ng, si - ng of the Ha - r - vest Wreath.

2) Sing, sing of the threshing of the corn.
   Sing, sing of the threshing of the corn.
   Sing of the barley, the wheat and the rye.
   Sing of the flail and the husks flying high.
   Sing, sing of the threshing of the corn.

3) Sing, sing of the cottage loaf baking.
   Sing, sing of the cottage loaf making.
   Sing of the water, the yeast and the flour.
   Sing of the egg yolk to cover it o'er.
   Sing, sing of the harvest loaf.

4) Sing, sing of the candle a-glowing.
   Sing, sing of the candle a-glowing.
   Sing of the fire, the wax and the tin.

Sing of the wick and the dipping in.
Sing, sing of the candle glow.

5) Sing, sing of the Christmas cake baking.
   Sing, sing of the Christmas cake making.
   Sing of the butter, the eggs and the flour.
   Sing of the icing that covers it o'er.
   Sing, sing of the Christmas cake.

6) Sing, sing of the honey cake baking.
   Sing, sing of the honey cake making.
   Sing of the honey, the eggs and the flour.
   Sing of the icing that covers it o'er.
   Sing, sing of the honey cake house.

Star Secrets

Margret Meyerkort

Twinkle, twinkle, little star,
How I wonder what you are?
Art a gateway in the sky?
Art a little angel's eye?
Shine your starry light to earth,
Bring a thousand stars to birth.
Stars in seed pod, apple, pear,
Stars in flowers everywhere.
So you guide me near and far,
Twinkle, twinkle, little star.

Sing to the tune of "Twinkle, Twinkle, Little Star."

Apple Secrets

Betty Jones

Who would think an apple
Red, gold, or green and round
Would have a secret deep inside
When cut it can be found!
I thought this secret only shone
In deep and darkest night
But when I cut my apple
It shines with five points bright!
And now you know the secret
Where shining stars are found
In every crunchy apple
Red, gold, or green and round.

*Cut open apples perpendicular to the stem
to find "star" inside, then quarter and give
pieces to children to enjoy. Try making
apple recipes in Autumn Cooking and Baking.*

My Nice Red Rosy Apple

Anonymous, words and music

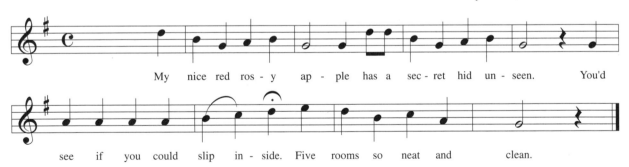

My nice red ros - y ap - ple has a sec - ret hid un - seen. You'd
see if you could slip in - side. Five rooms so neat and clean.

2) In each room there are living
   Two pips so black and bright.
   Asleep they are a-dreaming
   Of lovely warm sunlight.

3) And sometimes they are dreaming
   Of many things to be.
   How soon they will be hanging
   Upon the Christmas Tree.

Yellow the Bracken

Florence Hoatson, words ～ Traditional, music

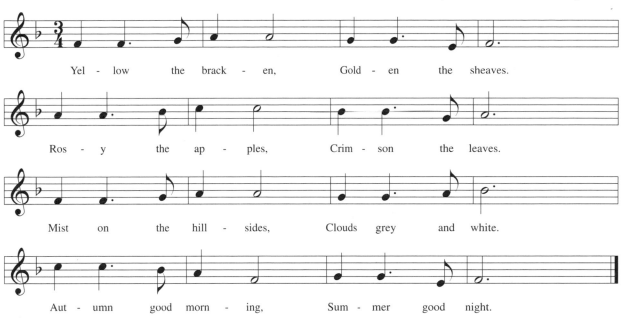

Yel - low the brack - en, Gold - en the sheaves.

Ros - y the ap - ples, Crim - son the leaves.

Mist on the hill - sides, Clouds grey and white.

Aut - umn good morn - ing, Sum - mer good night.

Wind Song

Betty Jones

Through the trees and over the plain
The wind sings its lonely refrain:
Ooh-ooh-ah-ooh-ooh!
It blows the leaves and through dried sheaves:
Ooh-ooh-ah-ooh-ooh!
O'er the sea it whips up the waves:
Ooh-ooh-ah-ooh-ooh!
Round the cliffs and through the caves:
Ooh-ooh-ah-ooh-ooh!

Oh, Brother Wind, you change your tune
From sad to happy to a gentle croon:
Ah-ah-ooh-ah-ah!
So sing me now to a restful sleep:
Ah-ah-ooh-ah-ah!
And blow me o'er the night-ocean deep:
Ah-ah-ooh-ah-ah
Where your voice and mine in silence keep:
Ah-ah-ooh-ah-ah-Sh-Sh-Sh...

End softly, and put index finger to lips in a
gesture for quiet.

Blow, Wind, Blow

Traditional

Blow, wind, blow!
And go, mill, go!
That the miller can grind his corn,
That the baker may take it,
And into bread make it,
And bring us a loaf in the morn,
And bring us a loaf in the morn.

Make pinwheels from Autumn Art and Hand-
work to represent windmills, or bake corncakes
from Autumn Cooking and Baking.

Silver

Walter de la Mare

Slowly, silently, now the moon
Walks the night in her silver shoon;
This way, and that, she peers, and sees
Silver fruit upon silver trees;
One by one the casements catch
Her beams beneath the silver thatch;
Couched in his kennel, like a log,
With paws of silver sleeps the dog;
From their shadowy cote the white
    breasts peep
Of doves in a silver-feathered sleep;
A harvest mouse goes scampering by,
With silver claws, and silver eye;
And moveless fish in the water gleam,
By silver reeds in a silver stream.

The Little Creature

Walter de la Mare

Twinkim, twankum, twirlum and twitch—
My great granddam—she was a witch;
Mouse in wainscot, saint in niche—
My great granddam—she was a witch;
Deadly nightshades flowers in a ditch—
My great granddam—she was a witch;
Long though the shroud, it grows stitch
   by stitch—
My great granddam—she was a witch;
Wean your weakling before you breech—
My great granddam—she was a witch;
The fattest pig's but a double flitch—
My great granddam—she was a witch;
Nightjars rattle, owls scritch—
My great granddam—she was a witch.

The Wise Old Owl

A wise old owl sat on an oak,
The more he heard, the less he spoke,
The less he spoke, the more he heard,
Why aren't we all like that wise bird?

Three Turkeys

1.The night be - fore Thanks-giv - ing, when I had gone to bed, I
5.Then on Thanks-giv - ing morn - ing, when the far - mer came a-round. Those

heard three tur - key gob - blers, and this is what they said:
thre - e tur - key gob - blers could n - ot b - e found.

Fine

2.The fi rst tur key said "I think that I will go, and

hide be hind the hay stack, where no one will know.

D.C. al Fine

Verses 3 and 4 are sung to the tune of verse 2.

3) The second turkey said, "I think I'll find a tree, and hide up in the branches, where no one will see."

4) The third turkey said, "I think it would be fun, to hide the farmer's hatchet, then run, run, run, run."

Thanksgiving Time

When all the leaves are off the boughs,
And nuts and apples gathered in,
And cornstalks waiting for the cows
And pumpkins safe in barn and bin,
Then Mother says, "My children dear,
The fields are brown and Autumn flies,
Thanksgiving Day is very near
And we must make Thanksgiving pies."

Autumn
Movement and Creative Drama

Old English Apple Picking

Here stands a good apple tree;
Stand fast at root, bear well at top,
Every little twig, bear an apple big,
Every little bough, bear an apple now.
Hats full! caps full! threescore sacks full!
Hullo, boys, hullo!

Stand straight.
Hands point to floor, rise above head.
Wiggle fingers of each hand.
Make fists.
Tap head with fists twice; clap three times.
Sling imaginary pack on back and trudge
around circle.

Mine Host of the "Golden Apples"
Thomas Westwood

A goodly host one day was mine,
A golden apple his only sign,
That hung from a long branch,
    ripe and fine.

My host was the bountiful apple tree;
He gave me shelter and nourished me
With the best of fare, all fresh and free.
And light-winged guests came not a few,
To his leafy inn, and sipped the dew,
And sang their best songs ere they flew.

I slept at night on a downy bed
Of moss, and my host benignly spread
His own cool shadow above my head.

When I asked what reckoning there
    might be,
He shook his broad boughs cheerily—
A blessing be thine, green apple tree!

One child is the Apple Tree with arms outstretched and fists for apples. Another child sits beneath the tree, while the tree gestures shelter and gives its fruit. One to three children flutter around tree and seated child; they sip dew, sing, and buzz (birds tweet, bees buzz, humming-birds hum). Child sleeps beneath tree boughs with arms crossed over heart. Tree shakes merrily with arms outstretched, fingers fluttering. Children seated in outer circle imitate all the gestures while the drama is enacted in the inside circle. Change actors and repeat.

Golden Apple Tree

Betty Jones

Begin by sitting in a circle with a tree-child standing in the center.

In the orchard, her branches spread wide,	*Tree-child spreads out arms.*
A golden apple tree, in whose leaves I hide	*Another child sits beneath tree.*
Cradled like a baby, her apples so sweet—	*Tree, with fists as apples, bends over child.*
I love to sit and eat, eat, eat!	*Child picks apples and eats.*
But when autumn winds begin to call,	*Wind-child whirls around tree and seated child.*
The leaves flutter down, turn colors and fall	*Children in circle flutter fingers overhead, then down.*
To Mother Earth where softly they lay	*Children in circle curl up as if sleeping.*
They invite me to come down from the branches and play,	*Children in circle kneel and beckon with their hands for child to leave the tree.*
And so I do, for my golden apple tree	*Child creeps from tree to circle.*
Becomes so bare, as bare can be!	*Children stretch fingers overhead.*
Yet still she spreads her branches as if to say,	*Tree sways entire body.*
"I'll wait for you with apples next year, okay?"	*Tree bows to children, and they bow to tree from kneeling position.*

Woodchoppers

We are working, working hard,
Chopping firewood in the yard.
Refrain: Chopping, chopping, chop,
    chop, chop!
Merrily the pieces drop!

Hands up high, that is right,
We must hold the chopper tight.
Refrain

It's the finest game we know,
It makes us warm from head to toe.
Refrain

Now a bundle we will tie,
We'll put it in the shed to dry.
Refrain

Standing in a circle, children grasp imaginary axes overhead and "chop" with large downward motions in rhythm. At "bundle," all stoop, pick up "heavy" bundle, trudge to center of circle, and dump the load of wood.

How the Leaves Came Down

Susan Coolidge

"I'll tell you how the leaves come down,"
The Great Tree to his children said:
"You're getting sleepy, Yellow and Brown,
Yes, very sleepy, little Red,
It's quite time now to go to bed."
"Ah," begged each silly, pouting leaf,
"Let us a little longer stay,
Dear Father Tree, behold our grief,
'Tis such a pleasant day,
We do not want to go away!"
So, just for one more merry day,
To the Great Tree the leaflets clung,
Frolicked and danced and had their way
Upon the autumn breezes swung,
Whispering all their sports among—
"Perhaps the Great Tree will forget
And let us stay until the spring,
If we beg and coax and fret."
But the Great Tree did no such thing;
He smiled to hear them whispering.
"Come children, all to bed," he cried;

And ere the leaves could urge their prayer,
He shook his head far and wide,
Fluttering and rustling everywhere,
Down sped the leaflets through the air.
I saw them; on the ground they lay,
Golden and red, a huddled swarm,
Waiting till one from far away,
White bedclothes heaped up her arm,
Should come to wrap them safe and warm.
The great bare tree looked down and
      smiled,
"Goodnight, dear little leaves," he said,
And from below each sleepy child
Replied, "Goodnight," and murmured,
"It is so nice to go to bed."

Act out similarly to Apple Tree, this time with three to five children as leaves. These verses can be an incentive before nap- or bedtime.

Stepping Stones

Stepping over stepping stones, one, two, three,
Stepping over stepping stones, come with me,
The river's very fast and the river's very wide,
So we'll step across the stepping stones
To reach the other side.

Meander in circle stepping on imaginary stepping stones in rhythm to words. Accentuate 1-2-3 and
"Come with me." Take little running steps for third line and slow to rhythmic walking for fourth line.
Jump to the "other side" at end of verse, change direction in circle, and repeat.

The River

But I can hear the river calling,
Calling loud and clear,
Stay a moment one and all,
You too will hear the river's call...
The river called softly
To the leaves on the tree,
"I'm waiting to take you
On a journey with me."
So leaves fell down softly
On that quiet autumn day,
And they floated with the river
Far, far away.

Children stand in two concentric circles.
Children in the outer circle make a listening
gesture with hand cupped around ear, while
children in inner circle hold hands and move in
one direction acting out river. Children in the
outer circle flutter their hands like falling leaves;
at the words "floated with the river" the river-
children take the hand of the leaf-child opposite.
Change circles and repeat in opposite direction.

The Northwind

The Northwind came along one day,
So strong and full of fun,
He called the leaves down from the trees
And said, "Run, children, run!"
They came in red and yellow dress,
In shaded green and brown,
And all the short November day,
He chased them round the town.

They ran in crowds, they ran alone,
They hid behind the trees,
The Northwind laughing found them there
And said, "No stopping, please!"
But when he saw them tired out

And huddled in a heap,
He softly said, "Goodnight, my dears,
Now let us go to sleep!"

*Dressed in autumn cape (orange, gold, or red)
the Northwind weaves in and out of children
seated in a circle. At "Run, children, run,"
Northwind gently taps three children and chases
them around circle; they hide in front of another
child seated in circle. Northwind taps them
again and says, "No stopping please!" The three
children jump up and run inside circle and
huddle in a heap at center. Northwind gently
pats their heads, covers them and himself with
cape, says, "Goodnight," and "sleeps."*

When Mary Goes Walking

Patrick Chalmers, words ∼ Margret Meyerkort, music

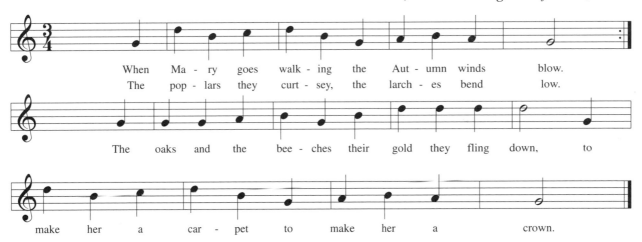

When Ma - ry goes walk - ing the Aut - umn winds blow.
The pop - lars they curt - sey, the larch - es bend low.

The oaks and the bee - ches their gold they fling down, to

make her a car - pet to make her a crown.

Children hold hands high standing in circle while Mary, or appropriate child's name, weaves in and out of circle during first verse. She then walks into center while children in circle let go of hands and all curtsey and bow to her. Each child holds his

hands up and flutters fingers downward while turning in place, then spreads out fluttering fingers in front of body and brings them upward to form crown on head.

Scary

Betty Jones

Begin standing in a circle.

Scary scarecrows? Ha, ha, ha!	*Make menacing scarecrow gesture.*
Crows just laugh at them! Caw, caw, caw!	*Flap arms like a crow and caw.*
Scary ghosties? Boo, boo, boo!	*Float arms up and down while turning in place.*
Not as scary as you, you, you!	*Point to someone else while making scary gesture.*
Scary witches? Hee, hee, hee!	*Fly on imaginary broomstick around circle.*
Not as scary as me, me, me!	*Stop in place and make scary gesture and sound.*

Old Mrs. Witch

Anonymous, words and music

2) Old Mrs. Witch, Old Mrs. Witch.
   Tell me what you see.
   Tell me what you see.
   I see a little Jack O' Lantern
   Looking at me.

3) Old Mrs. Witch, Old Mrs. Witch.
   Tell me what you'll do.
   Tell me what you'll do.
   I'll ride on my broomstick
   And I'll scare you.

Adult sings the first instance of any repeated phrase,
then child echoes.

Little Goblin

Anonymous, words and music

Run, lit- tle gob - lin, run a- long to mar - ket, run a - long to mar - ket, buy me a cow.
Gold, lit- tle gob- lin, not a pen- ny have I, make it by your mag - ic buy me a cow.
Buy me a brown cow, and a stool for milk - ing, and a li - ttle buck - et too, for the cream.
Run, lit- tle Gob- lin, run a- long to mar - ket, run a - long to mar - ket, buy me a cow.

*Sing while children run in time to the music with
furtive little goblin steps. Change direction at the
end of each verse.*

My Lantern

Anonymous, words and music

My lan - tern, my lan - tern, Sun and Moon and Star - light. In the dark- ened
My Lan- tern, my lan - tern, Sun and Moon and Star - light. Friend- ly lit - tle

heav - e - n high, Shine no stars with - in the sky. Dark - ened is the
lan - te - rn bright, be my Sun and shield this night. Be my moon and

path th - is night. With no Moon or Star as light.
sun s - o high. No light i - s in the sky.

*This song prepares children to go out with an adult
during any light festival, such as Halloween or
Michaelmas. Adults should always accompany and
supervise children with lit lanterns. Indoors, children
can practice walking in a circle, changing direction
after the first verse. See lantern-making in Autumn
Art and Handwork.*

Autumn Fingerplays and Riddles

Five Little Leaves

Five little leaves so bright and gay   *Hold out one hand; flutter outstretched fingers.*
Were dancing about a tree one day.   *Sway hand in rhythm overhead.*
The wind came blowing through the town,   *Put other hand to mouth and blow.*
    O-O-O-O
One little leaf came tumbling down!   *Sway hand from side to side while folding appropriate finger toward palm. Repeat entire verse and actions for 4-3-2-1.*

Autumn Leaves

Betty Jones

The trees are saying, "Goodbye" to their   *Stretch out arms and wave goodbye.*
    leaves
As they flutter and float and fly in the breeze.   *Flutter fingers.*
All golden, orange, and red, they sink softly   *Slowly bring fluttering fingers down to floor.*
    off to bed.
On Mother Earth's breast rests each   *Make sleeping gesture with palms together; give a big, restful sigh.*
    leafy head.

The Apple Tree

Here is an apple tree with leaves so green,   *Stretch arms, with fingers spread.*
Here are the apples that hang between,   *Make fists.*
When the wind blows, the apples will fall,   *Sway arms, then drop fists.*
Here is a basket to gather them all.   *Make large circle with arms in front of chest.*

The Squirrel

Whisky, frisky, hippity hop,
Up he goes to the treetop.   *Roll hands up and clap at top.*
Whirly, twirly, round and round,
Down he scampers to the ground.   *Roll hands down to lap.*
Furly, curly, what a tail,
Tall as a feather, broad as a snail.   *Bend arm in a crescent.*
Where's his supper? In the shell.   *Cup hands, look inside.*
Snap, crack, out it fell.   *Clap two times, open hands.*

Five Little Chipmunks

Betty Jones

Five little chipmunks by the lakeside shore,
One fell down and then there were four.
Four little chipmunks running wild and free,
One fell down and then there were three.
Three little chipmunks over logs they flew,
One fell down and then there were two.
Two little chipmunks they would race and run,
One fell down and then there was one.
One little chipmunk basking in the sun,
He went to his hollowed-home and then there were none!

*Extend fingers of one hand and fold toward palm, one at a time, as indicated
in verse. At the last line, place other hand on tummy with elbow held up;
tuck the last little chipmunk into this circle and then hide him under arm.*

Three Little Witches

One little, two little, three little witches,   *Hold up index, middle, then ring finger.*
Fly over haystacks, fly over ditches,   *Fly hand up and down.*
Slide down the moon without any hitches.   *Cup hand and scoop downward.*
Hey, ho, Halloween's here!   *Clap hands to the rhythm of the words.*

Five Little Pumpkins

Here's five little pumpkins sitting on a gate,	*Extend five fingers and sway hand side to side.*
The first one said, "Oh my, it's getting late!"	*Wiggle thumb.*
The second one said, "Oh, I don't care!"	*Wiggle index finger.*
The third one said, "There's something in the air!"	*Wiggle middle finger.*
The fourth one said, "Let's run, run, run!"	*Wiggle ring finger.*
The fifth one said, "It's only Halloween fun!"	*Wiggle little finger.*
Then WHOOSH goes the wind and OUT goes the light,	*Quickly extend hands and arms outward.*
And five little pumpkins roll out of sight!	*Bring arms to sides and make outward circling movements with hands.*

Scary Eyes

Betty Jones

Too-whit, too-whoo! the old owl spoke.	*Blink eyes while turning head.*
Hee-hee-hee! the witch sneered 'neath her cloak.	*Squint and look around with "cape" in front of face.*
Ooh-ooh-ooh! the ghost's scary eyes	*Make glasses around eyes with fingers.*
Look around for a big surprise.	*Peer around room mysteriously.*
Boo!	*Fly fingers outward.*

River

Runs all day and never walks,
Often murmurs, never talks,
It has a bed but never sleeps,
It has a mouth but never eats!

Autumn Games

The Friendly Ghost

Betty Jones

Begin by sitting in a circle with a ghost in center.

Am I a friendly ghost? Almost!	*Ghost floats about inner circle.*
I MIGHT be a friend to you!	*Ghost points to children in circle while floating by.*
But if a black bat or a hunched-back cat	*All children flap arms and hunch backs on all fours.*
Springs out, I'll yell SCAT and BOO!	*All jump up, all yell "scat" and "boo!"*

Pin the Nose (Hat, Mouth, Eyes, etc.) on the Jack-o'-lantern

Cut out a large orange pumpkin from felt or from paper and tack it on the wall. Cut out black features for the jack-o'-lantern and attach tape to the back of the forms. Blindfold each child, give them the forms, and let them tape the nose, etc., on the pumpkin to create a funny-faced jack-o'-lantern. The child who comes closest to placing the features appropriately, wins.

Jump the River

Place two sticks one foot apart to form a river. Children take turns jumping over. Widen the gap until one child wins by jumping the widest breadth of the river successfully and safely.

Wee Three Goblins

Betty Jones

Hoblins, goblins are we three.
Goofy, spoofy as can be!
With a twist about
And an in and out—
Children, you can't catch me!

Begin by standing in a circle, with plenty of space between children. Three goblins dance in the center, and the rest of the children also dance in their places.

At "a twist about," the goblins turn and dance toward the periphery. At "in and out," the goblins dance in and out between the children in the circle. At "can't catch me," each goblin taps a child in the outer circle, who then chases the goblin clockwise around the circle, all the way back to the tapped child's place. The tapped children become the next three goblins, and the verse and dance are repeated.

Autumn Art and Handwork

Autumn Leaves

Here are three fun activities children can do with fallen autumn leaves.

MATERIALS: Colored construction paper, tempera paints (yellow, orange, red, or brown), leaves with various sizes and shapes, block crayons, string

PROCEDURES: 1) Have the children paint the back of the leaves (vein side) with vivid tempera paints, turn painted side down, and press carefully onto a piece of construction paper to make leaf impression; lift leaf off by stem and dispose of in garbage (or allow paint to dry and use leaf for #3 below).

2) Arrange the leaves in various positions on a flat surface with vein side up. Place paper over leaves and rub the paper with the side of a crayon, pressing firmly without tearing paper, until a pattern of leaves appears. For variety, put color over color (beeswax block crayons blend well).

3) Collect autumn leaves and string together side by side by tying a knot around each stem; use for garlands, skirts, or tunics.

Pine Needle–Herb Dream Pillows

When you take a field trip or any simple nature walk, collect pine needles and other fragrant leaves (bay, eucalyptus) or herbs (lavender, rosemary, hops) and bring them back in a paper bag to dry.

MATERIALS: Various colors of felt cut into circles, diamonds, or crescent shapes (two per child); various colors of yarn; large sewing needles; cheese-cloth; leaves and herbs

PROCEDURE: Using colored yarn have the children freely stitch different designs on the two separate pieces of felt. Put a large handful of the dried herbs/leaves in the cheesecloth and tie securely. Place this between the two pieces of felt and have the children stitch around the border with a running stitch. To secure contents adult may loosely sew the border before the children do their stitching. At bedtime children place dream pillows on top of their regular pillows and breathe the fragrance while they sleep.

Crayon-Resist Ghost

MATERIALS: Construction paper; white wax crayon; tempera paint in black, dark blue, or purple

PROCEDURE: Children draw a "ghost picture" with a white wax crayon while pressing very hard. Brush dark paint over the entire paper. The ghost will resist the paint and show through. Boo!

Homemade Pinwheel

MATERIALS: Construction paper (or a watercolor painting), thumbtack with large plastic head, thin wooded dowel, scissors, tape

PROCEDURE: Fold a square piece of paper diagonally from corner to corner twice. Make sure the creases are sharp. Open paper, and, from each corner, draw cut-marks which curve towards the center of the paper. Leave the intersection of the folds unmarked. An adult should cut along these lines, then gently pull the four cut corner pieces to the center point. Overlap each of these points and tape lightly to hold them together. Tack through these corner points and the center point, then continue on to tack firmly to dowel. A child can then hold the dowel and blow through the "petals" to make the pinwheel turn.

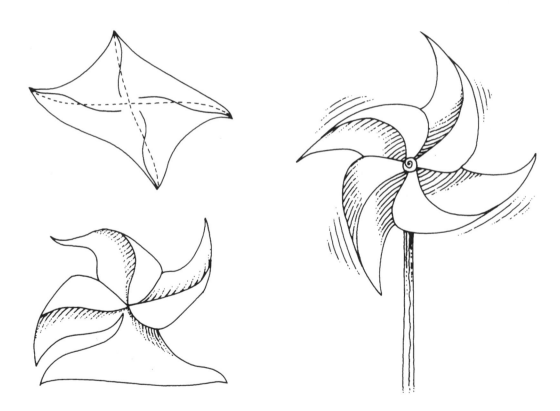

Lanterns

These lanterns are lovely for children's evening walks with their parents.

MATERIALS: A piece of 17-x-21-inch watercolor paper, watercolor paints (cobalt blue and red), scissors, tissue paper of various colors, glue, wire, tea candle (short votive in a metal container), double-sided tape to attach bottom of candle to base of lantern

PROCEDURE: Children paint on dry paper or use the wet-on-wet technique described on page 24 in "All Year Round." When dry, lay paper lengthwise; fold up approximately 1½ inches at bottom edge; open fold; clip bottom, at 1-inch intervals, toward fold. Help children cut out windows in various shapes, such as stars, diamonds, or moons. Cut out pieces of colored tissue to extend ¼ inch beyond cutout windows. On the unpainted side of the paper, spread glue, framing windows by ¼ inch. Press colored tissue into place.

Adult then helps the child roll paper into a tube and secure with double-sided tape at overlapping side seam. Holding tube over paper, trace two circles, and cut them out. Fold clipped edge to make bottom of tube. Spread glue on one side of each circle. Set tube on top of one circle, glue side up. Adult carefully lowers second circle, glue side down, to bottom of tube and presses into place. This forms a stable base for lantern. About 1 inch down from top of tube, poke holes on either side and reinforce holes with tape. Attach wire handle by inserting ends through holes and twisting at sides. Wrap tape around wire twists to secure. Attach several pieces of double-sided tape to underside of tea candle and press securely to center inside base.

Use only tea candles with metal cups and always supervise one-on-one when a child has a lighted lantern.

Thanksgiving Beads

MATERIALS: $1/2$ cup salt, 1 cup white flour, powdered tempera paint or food coloring, water, toothpicks, string

PROCEDURE: Mix the salt and the flour together. If color is desired, add paint or food coloring to water before mixing. Add water gradually until the mixture is of modeling consistency. Shape the mixture into beads of various shapes and sizes, like seasonal vegetables and fruits. Poke a hole through each bead with a toothpick before mixture dries. Let beads dry naturally. Thread beads on the string. Tie the string ends to form necklaces, bracelets, etc., for Thanksgiving feast celebrations.

Thanksgiving Pots

This is a way of giving thanks to the seasons and to the plant-world, and a way of honoring our relationship to and guardianship of this lifecycle. The children water and nurture a plant, which is Autumn's promise for Spring's birth.

MATERIALS: Clay, soil, flower bulbs

PROCEDURE: Flower pots can be made from clay by either coiling long rolled clay snakes into a pot form, or by pinching clay into a simple pinch pot. While the clay is still moist, children can inscribe their own symbol-messages on their pots. Lastly, make sure a small drainage hole is poked in the pot before firing. After firing, plant bulbs in the pot. Paper-white narcissus are the simplest, but daffodils and crocus can also be planted if bulbs are chilled in a paper bag in the refrigerator away from ripening fruit for 8 weeks. It will take 2–4 weeks for bulbs to grow; children will be able to give them as holiday gifts to their families. If firing clay pots is a problem, buy inexpensive plastic or terra-cotta pots, have the children decorate them with construction paper, glue, and marking pens, then plant as above.

Oatmeal Box Drum

Playing musical instruments enlivens the Thanksgiving or Harvest Festival.

MATERIALS: Oatmeal box, construction paper, glue, yarn, tape, 2 sticks

PROCEDURE: Place the lid on the empty oatmeal box and tape in place around cylinder. Cut construction paper so it is ½ inch shorter than height of oatmeal box. It should be long enough to wrap around cylinder, overlapping by 1 inch. Spread glue on cylinder and cover with construction paper, leaving ¼ inch of box exposed at top and bottom edges. Cut or draw designs to decorate drum. Glue yarn to cylinder to give a lacing effect. Use a coffee can or similar can with replaceable lid to create a different sound.

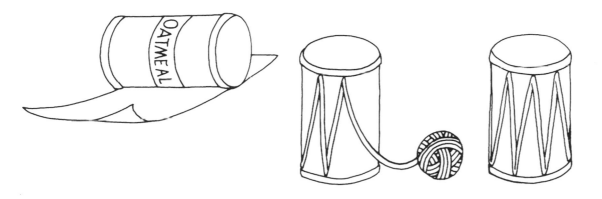

Salt Box Rattle

MATERIALS: Large cylindrical salt box, wooden stick, masking tape, construction paper, colored yarn, scissors, tiny stones

PROCEDURE: Cut construction paper to size and cover the sides of the salt box; tape side seams securely. Children can color designs on sides. Tape pour spout closed. Punch two holes exactly on opposite ends of box, centered, and be sure that the holes are the same size as the stick. With box turned on its side, place the stones inside. Insert the stick through the center holes. Fasten the stick with masking tape where it enters and exits the box. Decorate the stick with colored pieces of yarn and strong feathers, if available and desired.

Rolling Rattle

MATERIAL: Oatmeal box or coffee tin, dried beans or peas, masking tape, construction paper

PROCEDURE: Follow Salt Box Rattle instructions, without poking holes in box. Fill with dried beans or peas. Seal top of rattle with tape; roll it, kick it, shake it, pound it!

Paper-Strip Weaving

MATERIALS: Two pieces of $8^1/_2$-x-11-inch construction paper, block crayons, scissors, glue, clear contact paper to cover and protect (optional)

PROCEDURE: Using the broad side of the crayons, color horizontal stripes across length of one paper and vertical stripes across length of other piece of paper. Fold the horizontally striped paper in half and cut along the stripes at 1-inch intervals from the fold to within 1 inch of the outer edge. Open and lay flat. Cut vertical stripes (at least 1 inch wide) for strips to weave in and out of horizontally cut paper, alternating the in and out pattern for each strip. Help children to nestle the paper strips side by side as they weave the strips from one end of the paper to the opposite border. Glue to secure both ends of the vertical strips when completed. Cover with contact paper to preserve this weaving as a placemat for the children for their Thanksgiving, Harvest, or other festival feasts.

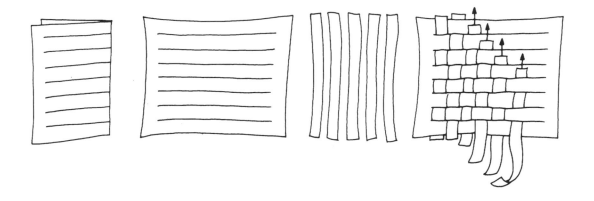

Corn Husk Dolls

Corn Husk Dolls are symbols of the Earth Mother, or of the Earth Child. They can be given as gifts, or they make lovely decorations. This is a craft that requires a lot of adult help.

MATERIALS: Dry cornhusks, sheep's wool, embroidery thread, pipe cleaners

PROCEDURE: Soak cornhusks in water for 1/2 hour, or until they become flexible. Form a bit of wool into a 3/4-inch-diameter ball. Place the wool ball in the middle of a broad piece of cornhusk. Fold husk end to end. Tuck in cornhusk edges around ball and tie with thread just below husk-enfolded ball (1). Make the pipe cleaner the same length as the folded cornhusk by bending each of its ends and twisting the excess back around itself. Wrap a little wool around the pipe cleaner and then roll a narrow length of cornhusk around it. Tie securely 1/4 inch from each end (2). Take a bit of wool and fold it over the middle of husk-wrapped pipe cleaner. This will help form the torso (3).

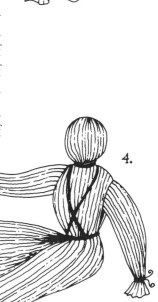

Now spread open the cornhusk containing the wool ball and place the pipe cleaner husk across it, right up against the tied ball. Fold the cornhusk closed again and tie securely first under crosspiece to form the waist at the base of the wool torso; then with the same thread, crisscross at front, go over shoulders, crisscross at back, and come back around to the front, tying securely at waist. Make legs by gently splitting cornhusk in two, lengthwise. Then bend back and twist one end of a pipe cleaner so that it is about 3/4 of an inch longer than the leg needs to be. Wrap the pipe cleaner in wool, leaving 3/4 of an inch exposed at one end. Insert unwrapped end into doll body. Fold half of the cornhusk around the pipe cleaner and tie securely at ankle. Repeat procedure for the other leg. Bend pipe cleaner at ankles to make feet. Make a skirted doll (with or without legs) by folding lengths of cornhusks over a piece of thread and tying skirt around doll's waist (4). Let dry.

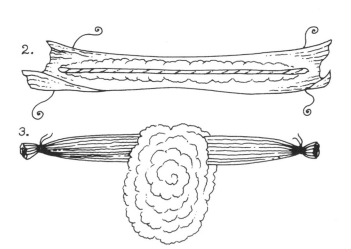

Autumn Cooking and Baking

Apple Sauce

> 3 pounds (approximately 10 medium-size) apples
> Honey or sugar (brown or white)
> Cinnamon (optional)

Wash, cut (through middle to find star secret!), and core apples (or give one apple per child if doing this activity with a whole group). Cut apples into quarter pieces or chunks and place them in a saucepan; partly cover with water. Simmer until tender. Put cooked apples through a food mill or grinder, or mash them with a fork or potato masher. Add honey or sugar to taste and stir well, cooking gently for 3 minutes. Cool and sprinkle cinnamon on top if desired.

Corncakes

> 3 tablespoons honey
> 2 cups warm water (110° F)
> 1 tablespoon yeast
> 2$\frac{1}{2}$ to 3 cups cornmeal
>
> 2$\frac{1}{2}$ to 3 cups whole wheat flour
> 1$\frac{1}{2}$ teaspoons salt
> 1 ear corn (optional)
> $\frac{1}{8}$ cup oil

In a large bowl, dissolve honey in warm water and gently stir in yeast; set aside to rise while mixing all the dry ingredients in another bowl. An adult should scrape kernals off corn on the cob and gently stir into liquid along with oil. Mix dry ingredients with wet to form dough. Knead the dough on a floured board until pliable. Divide the dough into ten parts. Children can knead their dough, pat, and fork initials on top. Allow dough to rise 1 hour in a warm place, covered with clean tea towel. Bake in a preheated 350° F oven for $\frac{1}{2}$ hour. Use this recipe to create Corncake Men, and make up stories about them at Thanksgiving or Harvest Feasts.

Candied Apples

Mixed nuts, crushed
  (walnut, peanuts, almonds, etc.)
Shredded coconut
Seeds (sunflower, pumpkin, etc.)
Dried fruit, chopped
  (fine dates, raisins, apricots, etc.)

Popsicle™ sticks as holders
Cold apples (1 per child)
Honey (1/4 cup per child)

Mix nuts, coconut, seeds, and fruit together in a shallow pan. Adult should insert a Popsicle™ stick through the core of each apple. Holding the stick, child dips an apple into the honey, letting excess drip off before rolling apple firmly in fruit and nut mixture. If not eaten right away, put candied apples on wax paper in the refrigerator to keep cold.

Popcorn Balls

3 quarts popcorn, freshly
  popped using 1/4 cup oil
  and 1/2 cup popcorn
1 cup light corn syrup

1 cup sugar
1/2 teaspoon salt
1 teaspoon vanilla

An adult should pop the popcorn and cook the sugar mixture, closely supervising children while making this recipe. Keep popped popcorn warm in 330° F oven. Combine corn syrup, sugar, and salt in a heavy 2-quart saucepan. Cook and stir over medium heat until the mixture comes to a boil. Cook without stirring for 4 minutes. Remove from the heat. Stir in the vanilla and mix well. Pour syrup slowly over popped corn in a fine stream. Mix with a wooden spoon. When cool enough to handle, but still warm, shape into 2- to 2½-inch balls. Makes 12 to 18 balls. (While popping the popcorn sing with the children to the tune of "Row, Row, Row the Boat": "Pop, pop, pop the corn, pop it big and white, popping, popping, popping, popping, 'til it is just right!")

Pumpkin Seeds

2 cups dried pumpkin seeds
2 tablespoons melted butter

$^1/_2$ teaspoon Worcestershire
    or soy sauce
Salt

To obtain seeds, clean out pumpkins that are going to be carved into jack-o'-lanterns. Wash seeds thoroughly and let them dry naturally in a sunny window for a few days. When ready to proceed, melt butter. Combine butter with the Worcestershire or soy sauce, and spread lightly over bottom of large baking pan. Coat pumpkin seeds by spreading and turning them on pan. Sprinkle salt to taste. Bake in a preheated 250° F oven, stirring occasionally, until the seeds are crisp and brown (approximately 2 hours).

Simple Pie Crust

4 cups flour
1$^1/_2$ cups butter
$^1/_2$ teaspoon salt

$^3/_4$ cup ice water (20 tablespoons
    for children to dip, pour, and
    count!)

Mix the flour, butter, and salt together and add the water, slowly stirring with a fork. Roll dough out on a floured piece of wax paper with a floured rolling pin. Put upside-down pie tin in the center of the dough and cut dough at least 1$^1/_2$ inches larger than the pie tin. Carefully lift under wax paper and gently turn pie tin upright. Remove wax paper and press pie crust into the tin; prick bottom crust with fork for airholes and pinch extra dough around outer edges. Preheat 350° F oven and bake shell(s) 15 minutes before filling. Makes three or four 9-inch pie crusts or 3 to 4 dozen individual tart shells. (To make tart shells: cut thinly rolled dough in circles and press into greased, large-size muffin tins. Prevent shells from bubbling by weighting down with dried beans or ceramic pie weights.)

Apple Pie

2 apples per child   Honey
Pinch of cinnamon   Squeeze of lemon

An adult should cut apples in half through midsection to find the star and closely supervise children while they cut small pieces from these half-sections. (Turn the apple pieces on their flat sides for easier cutting; use only dull kitchen knives with small children.) Children place their apple pieces into individual pie shells, or into a 9-inch pie shell, to the top edge; sprinkle with cinnamon, drizzle honey, and squeeze a little lemon juice over top of apples. Adult cuts a top crust to fit; children pinch crusts together at edge. Adult pricks top of crust with child's initials. Bake in preheated 350° F oven until golden brown (approximately 45 minutes).

Pumpkin Pie

3 eggs   2 teaspoons cinnamon
1/2 cup honey   1 teaspoon salt
1/4 cup molasses   1 1/2 cups milk
1 teaspoon ginger   2 1/2 cups pumpkin (1 large can)
1 teaspoon nutmeg

Beat the eggs well with whisk; add other ingredients in the order given. Fill bottom pie crust until just below rim. Bake in preheated 350° F oven for 80 to 90 minutes (until knife comes out clean when center of pie is pierced.) This recipe will fill two 9-inch pie shells or approximately 2 dozen individual pie shells.

November Nectar

For a delicious seasonal beverage, chill a pitcher of apple cider. Before serving, add apple slices and a dash of cinnamon.

No-Cook Cranberry Sauce

1 medium orange
1 package (12 ounces) fresh,
    whole cranberries, washed

$3/4$ to 1 cup sugar (to taste)

Slice orange into eighths and remove seeds. Put cranberries and orange pieces into a bowl and mix together. Put large spoonfuls of fruit into hand-turned food grinder to evenly chop into bowl set below mouth of grinder. When all fruit has been ground, stir in sugar to taste. Store in refrigerator or freeze for later use; makes approximately $2\frac{1}{2}$ cups. This recipe can be made in a food processor. If so, be careful not to liquify fruit as it is best if it is coarsely chopped and allowed to sit for at least 1 hour before eating.

Winter

King Winter rules throughout the land "with his bold, and mighty, frosty hand," or does he? If you live in the tropics, perhaps it's balmy and breezy at this time of year, and holly is certainly not the seasonal flower! Children benefit and appreciate festivals most when they are adapted to fit their natural surroundings. Christmas is a holiday celebrated worldwide and cross-culturally. The light festivals of Hanukkah, Kwanzaa, and the Winter Solstice all carry the essence of the Universal Light in their celebration. Now is a time to be mindful of the kingdoms of Nature. Are the stones and plants and animals asleep or awake? What is the mood of Nature? What are the elemental beings doing? How can we aid these fairies, elves, and gnomes on behalf of our dear Mother Earth?

As the drops of rain or snowflakes fall, or the sunbeams play, families and friends rejoice through the Solstice, Hanukkah, Christmas, and Kwanzaa celebrations with their promise of the light of spring and new birth. Celebrate truly with the children this winter-tide.

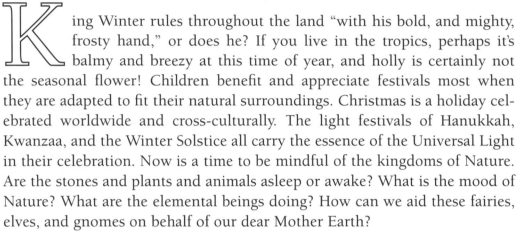

Winter Verses and Poems

Rain

Robert Louis Stevenson

The rain is raining all around,
It falls on field and tree,
It rains on the umbrellas here,
And on the ships at sea.

The Rain

Up above the rain clouds tumble
And in the merry rush and tumble,
Raindrops downward dance and spatter,
Pitter-patter, pitter-patter.
Stormwinds send the clouds a-whirling,
Rain comes rushing, swishing, swirling,
Raindrops downwards dance and spatter,
Pitter-patter, pitter-patter.

Winter

William Shakespeare

When icicles hang by the wall,
And Dick the Shepherd blows his nail,
And Tom bears logs into the hall,
And milk comes frozen home in pail;
When blood is nipped and ways be foul,
Then nightly sings the staring owl,
To-whit, to-whoo,
A merry note,
While greasy Joan doth keel the pot.
When all aloud the wind doth blow,
And coughing drowns the parson's saw;
And birds sit brooding in the snow,
And Marian's nose is red and raw;
When roasted crabs hiss in the bowl,
Then nightly sings the staring owl,
To-whit, to-whoo,
A merry note,
While greasy Joan doth keel the pot.

Jolly Old St. Nicholas

Traditional, words and music

Jol - ly Old St. Ni - cho - las, Lean your ear this way.
When the clock is strik - ing twelve, when I'm fast a - sleep.

Don't you tell a sin - gle soul what I'm going to say.
Down the chim - ney broad and black, with your pack you'll creep.

Christ - mas Eve is com - ing soon, now you dear old man,
All the stock - ings you will find, hang - ing in a row.

Whis - per what you'll bring to me, tell me if you can.
Mine will be the short - est one, you'll be sure to know.

Snowflakes

Wendalyn von Meyenfeldt

The snowflake fairies weave and spin
A cloak to wrap Earth Mother in,
With crystal shine and starry thread,
They crown with diamonds her sleepy head.
The snowflake fairies spin and weave
In wintertime a sweet reprieve,
With starry thread and crystal shine,
They promise Earth of worlds divine.

Winter's Mood

Betty Jones

All outside is dark and cold
But just beneath the earth
Sleep seeds from which new life springs
Bringing Nature's gifts to birth.

Buttercups and Daisies

Mary Howitt

Buttercups and daisies,
Oh the pretty flowers,
Coming ere the springtime,
To tell of sunny hours.
While the trees are leafless,
While the fields are bare,
Buttercups and daisies
Spring up here and there,
Ere the snowdrop peepeth
Ere the crocus bold
Ere the early primrose
Opens its paley gold
Somewhere on a sunny bank.
Buttercups are bright,
Somewhere 'mong the frozen grass,
Peeps the daisy white.

Like hardy flowers
Like to children poor
Playing in their sturdy health
By their mother's door.
Purple with the North Land
Yet alert and bold;
Fearing not and caring not,
Though they be a-cold!
What to them is winter!
What are stormy showers!
Buttercups and daisies
Are these human flowers!
He who gave them hardships
And a life of care,
Gave them likewise hardy strength
And patient hearts to bear.

Midwinter Night

Margret Meyerkort, words ~ Anonymous, music

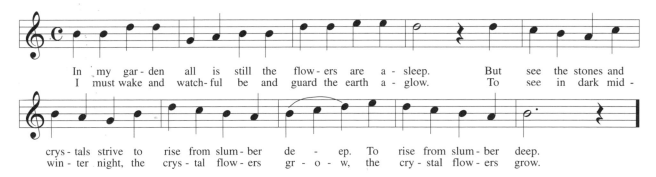

In my gar-den all is still the flow-ers are a-sleep. But see the stones and
I must wake and watch-ful be and guard the earth a-glow. To see in dark mid-

crys-tals strive to rise from slum-ber de - ep. To rise from slum-ber deep.
win-ter night, the crys-tal flow-ers gr-o-w, the cry-stal flow-ers grow.

Winter Movement and Creative Drama

Wintertime

Betty Jones

Begin by standing in a circle.

Oh, hear the winds call,	*Raise hand to mouth and sound out "wooo."*
Listen to the nuts fall,	*Snap fingers.*
See the squirrel gather its food,	*Flutter fingers and reach forward, make gathering gesture.*
To bed goes the bear,	*Lumber around in a circle.*
All creatures prepare	*Stop, all hold hands, and sit down in place.*
For the wintertime mood.	*While holding hands, raise hands upward.*
Soft snow falls at night	*Everyone flutter fingers downward to floor.*
Covering the earth crystal-white,	*Spread fingers outward away from body.*
While all are snug in bed,	*Place hands together in sleeping gesture, eyes closed.*
But with the sunrise	*Eyes stay closed; arms sweep upward overhead.*
Children open their eyes	*Open eyes; stretch hands upward, fingertips meeting.*
To play in the snow instead!	*Children rise in circle, rub hands together.*
The air is so clear!	*Stretch hands upward again, take a deep breath, exhale.*
Wrapped in warm winter gear,	*Pretend to dress in winter clothes.*
Out to the snow we go!	*Pretend to trudge through snow around circle.*
Jack Frost bites the nose	*Stop trudging and pinch nose.*
And soon freezes our toes!	*Bend down; rub toes to warm them.*
Now starts this wintertime show!	*Stand and turn around in place; extend arms outward from sides in gesture of gratitude.*

The Kind Mousie

Natalie Joan

There once lived a cobbler and he was wee,
He lived in a hole of a very big tree.
He had a good neighbor and she was a mouse,
She did his wee washing and tidied his house.
Each morning at seven he heard a wee tap,
And in came the mouse in her apron and cap.
She lit a small fire and she fetched a wee broom,
She swept and she polished his little, wee room.
To take any wages she'd always refuse,
So the cobbler said, "Thank You!" and mended her shoes.

Children act out Mouse's chores throughout verse with one child playing the cobbler.

Snowflakes

Traditional, words and music

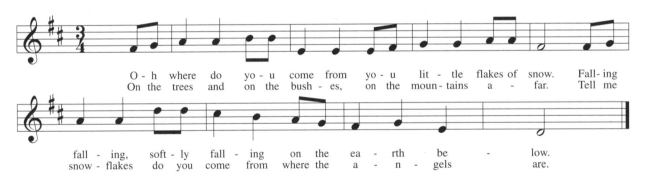

O - h where do yo - u come from yo - u lit - tle flakes of snow. Fall- ing
On the trees and on the bush - es, on the moun - tains a - far. Tell me

fall - ing, soft - ly fall - ing on the ea - rth be - low.
snow - flakes do you come from where the a - n - gels are.

1st verse: Begin by standing in a circle; flutter fingers overhead while turning in place. Flutter fingers downward; stoop to floor.

2nd verse: Rise and spread arms upwards as trees; make ring with arms with fingers touching. Flutter fingers overhead while turning in place.

Shivering, Quivering

Betty Jones

Shivering, quivering, freezing cold,	*Hug self and shiver both body and voice.*
Rub your hands, then your arms hold. BRRR!	*Rub hands and arms.*
Shivering, quivering, frosty as ice,	*Hug self and shiver.*
Rub your feet hard, at least once or twice!	*Rub one foot, then the other.*
BRRR!	
Shivering, quivering, blow out your air,	*Shiver, exhale loudly.*
Take a deep breath and blow it out there!	*Breathe deeply, exhale loudly.*
BRRR-BRRR-BRRR!	

Snowy Day

Begin by standing in a circle.

This is how the snowflakes play about,	*Dance in toward center of a circle, then back*
Up in cloudland they dance in and out.	*to original places.*
This is how they whirl down the street,	
Powdering everybody that they meet.	*Turn in place with fingers fluttering overhead.*
This is how they come fluttering down,	
Whitening the roads, fields, and town.	*Float fluttering fingers downward; sit in place.*
This is how the snowflakes cover the trees,	*Flutter fingers overhead.*
Each branch and twig bends in the breeze.	*Bend arms and hands.*
This is how the snowflakes blow in a heap,	*Blow on fluttering fingers and make a heap in*
Looking just like fleecy sheep.	*front of self with arms; hold still.*
This is how they cover the ground,	*Fingers flutter to ground, arms make spreading*
Cover it thickly without a sound.	*gesture in front of body.*
This is how the people shiver and shake	*Cross arms and make shivering motions with*
On a snowy morning when they first awake.	*entire body.*
This is how the snowflakes melt away	*Flutter fingers, spread arms; rise and make*
When the sun sends out his beams to play.	*a circle overhead with arms.*

Chestnuts

Swinging, swinging, little chestnut cradles,
Swinging, swinging, in the branches high,
Still in the night, stars twinkle bright,
Jack Frost runs soft o'er fields of white,
He nips at the cradles with fingers of ice,
Down fall the chestnuts all in a thrice,
Down fall the cradles and split open, POP!
And brown baby chestnuts all out of
    them hop,
Down in the warm earth they all sink to nest,
Sleep, baby chestnuts, on Mother Earth's
    breast,
Sleep 'til the spring sun climbing the skies,
Shines through the darkness and bids you
    arise!

Make swaying, cradling motion with arms.
Sway with arms stretched overhead.
Step in to shrink circle, then out to enlarge it.
Walk briskly on tip-toes around circle.
Stand still; pinch air with right hand, left, right.
Fingers flutter downward.
Jump and land with feet apart.
Jump and land with feet together.

Kneel slowly.
Make sleeping gesture, while crouching.

Rise slowly.
Extend arms and make a ring with fingertips
    meeting.

Knock, Knock Gnomes

Betty Jones

Knock, knock gnomes, in our homes
Of stony rock, we knock, knock, knock!
To make our way, to the light of day,
For shining light makes our gems bright!
Seeds will grow, reflect and show
The colors of our good Mother Earth!

*Begin by crouching in a circle. Tap one fist on
top of the other alternately while all slowly rise
until upright. End by fluttering fingers high
overhead to reflect colors while turning in place.*

Groundhog Day

Betty Jones

Begin by sitting in a circle.

Bears hug in their caves so snug.   *Hug self with eyes closed; smile.*

Bears hug in their caves so snug.	*Hug self with eyes closed; smile.*

Squirrels are restless in their hollow
   tree.
	*Make hole with one hand, wiggle fingers of other
	   hand through hole.*

Fox family yawns and stretches in their lair.	*Yawn and stretch limbs.*

Groundhog pokes his head from
   the ground,
	*Make large ring with arms and poke head
	   through.*

Whiffs and sniffs and looks around.	*Sniff, look around through hole.*
Will or won't his shadow be found?	*Nod head "yes," then "no," shrug shoulders.*
If it is, we all will know	*Nod "yes" and rise to squat position.*
Spring is getting ready to go!	*Spring up in place with outstretched limbs.*

Radiant Sun

Betty Jones

*Give children colored veils, or assign each child
a flower based on the color of her clothing.*

Radiant Sun from his throne in the sky	*Sun child sits on chair.*

Looked down on earth where sleeping
   seeds lie
	*Seed children huddle around sun making sleeping
	   gesture under their veils.*

And thought to himself, "I think it's time	*Sun looks at wristwatch.*
For flower babies to wake up and play."	*Sun points to the seed children.*

So with his rays of gold he knocked and
   knocked
	*Sun pretends to knock on door above each
	   sleeping seed.*

At each and every flower family's door,	

"Wake up! Wake up!" he chuckled
   with glee,
	*Sun places hands around mouth in a calling
	   gesture.*

"Time to wake up and color Earth's floor!"	*White-, orange-, and red-veiled children rise and stretch.*
The snowdrops were first, then crocus and rosies,	
Daffodils, violets and all sorts of posies	*Yellow- and violet-veiled children rise.*
Yawning and stretching under Radiant Sun,	*All turn in place, stretch arms up.*
Yes, all we flowers create springtime fun!	*All flutter fingers, skip around circle; sun stands and rotates in place, arms out, fluttering fingers.*

Winter Fingerplays and Riddles

Snowmen

Betty Jones

Five little snowmen stand up tall,   *Hold up one hand with fingers extended.*
Their bodies are round, their heads are   *Make circle with arms in front of body,*
     snowballs.   *then make smaller circle a bit higher.*
Five little snowmen would walk if they   *Walk two fingers of one hand on palm of other*
     could   *hand.*
To the shade of the trees or the shelter of   *Make roof gesture by touching tips of fingers*
     the wood,   *together overhead.*
For five little snowmen know when   *Make circle overhead for sun.*
     Father Sun's around
They won't last long 'cuz they'll melt on   *Bring circle down slowly and spread arms out*
     the ground!   *in front of body.*

Snowy Hill

Betty Jones

On this hill, the snow you see,   *Incline one arm down, and stroke it with the other hand.*
Here's my sled and here is me!   *Extend other hand and wiggle thumb for "me."*
Ready, ho! Down I go!   *Slide sled hand down hill arm from shoulder to fingertips.*
So fast, so fun, yippee!   *Wiggle thumb vigorously at end.*

Lighted Candle

Little Nancy Etticoat,
In a white petticoat and a red nose;
The longer she stands
The shorter she grows.

Ask children to guess what Little Nancy is,
then carefully light a white candle to show them.

Rain Riddle

I have been to earth before,
I have stopped many children's games,
You have walked in my puddles,
Can you guess my name?

It's Raining

Betty Jones

Pitter patter, pitter patter, pitter patter, plop!	*Tap thumb to fingers in rhythm, clap at "plop."*
Pitter patter, pitter patter, outside the raindrops drop!	*Repeat tapping motion but begin overhead and move downward, clap at "drop."*
Every little bit of rain splashes on my windowpane,	*Repeat tapping motion, waving hand side to side.*
Pitter patter, pitter patter, will you ever stop?	*Tap fingers while moving hand around body.*
Pitter patter, pitter patter, oh so many hours!	*Tap fingers while moving hand up and down.*
Pitter patter, pitter patter, I know you're good for flowers,	*Tap fingers, then cup hands; wiggle fingers upward.*
But when you come everyday, I can't go outside to play!	*Tap fingers overhead, then move downward; shake head "no."*
Pitter patter, pitter patter, please now stop your showers!	*Tap fingers, end in a prayer gesture.*

Working Gnomes

We hammer and knock	*Hammer fist on fist, moving up from chest.*
On hard stony rock	*Continue hammering above head.*
For a path we would make	*Extend arms straight out in front.*
For the starlight to take	*Raise arms upward.*
That the stars they may shine	*Flutter fingers overhead.*
With their love so divine.	*Continue to flutter fingers and sway arms.*
We push down with the roots,	*Hold index fingers parallel, point downward.*
And push up with the shoots	*Point index fingers up and push upward.*
'Til to daylight they rise,	*Open up fingers and reach wide overhead.*
Free to grow toward the skies.	*Flutter fingers and sway arms overhead.*

Winter Games

Stir the Soup

Children are seated in a circle. One child stands in the center with a stick. There are just enough chairs for all except the player with the stick. The seated children stand and walk in one direction around the inside of the circle to the rhythm of "stir the soup." This is repeated continuously while the child in the center stirs with the stick. Suddenly, he taps the floor three times, drops the stick and runs for a seat. The child left without a seat becomes the next to stir the soup.

Old Mother Cat

This is a fun indoor game when the weather is bad. Everyone gets on their hands and knees. One person is the cat, the rest are mice. Mother Cat says as she slowly moves her head: "I'm the cat of this snug little house and I am looking for a mouse. House-mouse, cat-rat, I'm coming to see just where you're at!" Immediately, the cat starts crawling after the mice, while the mice crawl away from her. The mouse she tags is the next cat and the next cat says the rhyme and chases the mice, etc. Cat and mice may crawl anywhere designated.

Winter Art and Handwork

Wreath

MATERIALS: Clothes hanger or other heavy wire made into round hoop (or premade hoops from hardware store), florist wire for attaching boughs, string to attach decorative pieces (pine cones, holly berries, dried flowers, red or other festive colored ribbons for bows), fir boughs cut into pieces for bunching, bay branches for scent (if desired)

PROCEDURE: Take a bunch of fir stems and attach firmly to wire hoop with florist wire. Make another bunch and overlap cut ends of the first bunch so that the wire is hidden. Proceed in one direction until the wreath is covered. Then attach decorative pieces to wreath with string. If wreath is for laying on a table, an adult can make candle holders by coiling a heavy wire around base of candle and securing firmly to wreath wire base. An adult should always closely supervise a lit candle. If the wreath is for hanging, omit candle and attach a wire to the back of the wreath.

Holiday Greetings

MATERIALS: Red, green, blue, and white construction paper; crayons; glue; scissors; gold stars

PROCEDURE: Place a rectangular piece of white paper on top of a colored piece of the same size. Fold the papers so that the side edges meet in the middle to create a gatefold or "door" effect. Cut the top of the folded paper in an arch shape. Glue the white piece inside the colored paper. Write an invitation or child's holiday greeting inside the card. The child can draw or color on the interior sides. Close door of card with a gold star.

Candle Making

MATERIALS: Clean commercial beeswax, candlewick, tin cans, double boiler, newspaper to spread on floor, pencil, cord strung between two walls, candle decorating wax if available

PROCEDURE: Place newspaper on the floor for protection. An adult should warm beeswax in a can in a double boiler; wax should be thoroughly melted but not boiling. Cut the wick 3 inches longer than the desired length of finished candle. Wrap one end of the wick around the end of the pencil and have child hold the opposite end of the pencil out so that wick hangs straight down. An adult should supervise children as they dip the wick into the can of warm wax and then walk slowly around table in one direction while singing seasonal favorites or listening to festive music in the background before dipping their candle again. Continue dipping and walking around the table carefully until the candle is the desired thickness. Hang over an inside clothesline to dry. After candles cool and harden, colored candle decorating wax can be cut into seasonal shapes and pressed onto them.

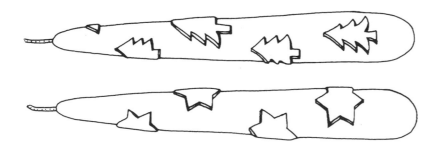

Wool Angels

MATERIALS: White wool fleece, gold thread, gold star

PROCEDURE: Take a piece of clean white wool that has been carded smooth (approximately 1 foot in length). Tie a firm knot in the middle of the wool to form a head. Gently separate and pull half the amount of wool that's left on either side of the head and tie it off at the waist with gold thread to form the lower body, leaving the remainder of the wool fleece as wings. Lightly tease this wool, spreading the fibers into the shape of wings, and sew to maintain shape with as few stitches as possible, securing the wings to the angel's back. Attach a star on angel's forehead, if desired.

Christmas Tree Chains

Here are two great ways to make chains:

MATERIALS: Brightly colored paper strips, approximately 6 inches long and 1 inch wide; glue

PROCEDURE: Glue ends of one paper strip together to form loop, then link with the next paper strip and continue in this manner to create a chain.

MATERIALS: Popped popcorn, needle and thread, cranberries (optional)

PROCEDURE: String the popcorn piece by piece until chain is desired length; cranberries can be added to brighten up the white popcorn chain.

Potato Print Wrapping Paper

MATERIALS: Shelf paper, poster paint, paint brushes, potato, paring knife, holiday or other cookie cutters

PROCEDURE: Allow each child to choose a design. Adult should cut the design in a halved potato. The design can be cut freehand, using the paring knife, or an impression can first be made with the cookie cutter and carved around with the paring knife. Make the impression at least ¼ inch deep to provide form in relief when you have cut away the outside edges. Each child brushes paint on his relief shape and uses it to stamp a piece of wrapping paper. Let dry. Children can trade potatoes to make extra-special wrapping paper.

Snowflakes

MATERIALS: White tissue paper precut into circles or squares, scissors

PROCEDURE: Children fold paper in half twice, then snip pieces from edges or gently tear irregular pieces. Unfold. Place snowflakes in the window so the sun shines through them. If the children are good with scissors, they can experiment with cutting through more folds of the paper.

Whipping Snow

MATERIALS: Ivory flakes, egg beater, mixing bowl, water, dark-colored construction paper, paper cups

PROCEDURE: In mixing bowl, combine Ivory flakes and water in a 2:1 ratio, and beat (consistency should be thick). Give the children paper cups filled with the whipped snow and let them fingerpaint on the paper using the snow as paint. If the snow is very thick, try making snow sculptures and little snowmen.

Gnome Pouch

MATERIALS: Various colors of felt and yarn, large needles

PROCEDURE: Cut pieces of felt in the shape indicated. Give two pieces to each child and show them how to stitch freely with different colors of yarn. Encourage diamond, ruby, or sapphire shapes (which can be sewn or cut from felt and sewn on). When both sides are covered with jewels, children stitch both sides together around the border. For a handle, they can make a twizzle by taking two long pieces of yarn, two children holding either end and twisting the yarn in opposite directions until it is very taut. An adult then pinches and holds the mid-point as the children join ends. Adult knots the ends while one child holds her finger at mid-point. Another child takes knotted end and says, "Let go." The yarn will dance as it twists into a cord to sew onto the pouch.

Gnomes and Dwarves

MATERIALS: Various colors of felt and yarn, large needles, white fleece

PROCEDURE: Fold a square piece of felt in half. Cut as directed, with the neck opening half as long as the vertical head opening. With a blanket stitch, sew closed the opening along the top. With a running stitch, sew along the neck line, leaving enough yarn at the beginning and end to tie securely. Stuff the head with a ball of fleece. Tightly gather the loose yarn ends to form the head; tie ends in a bow. Pull some of the fleece out of the head as a beard. (You can blanket stitch the long front opening and stuff the body for a firm standing dwarf, or keep the body empty for a puppet dwarf.)

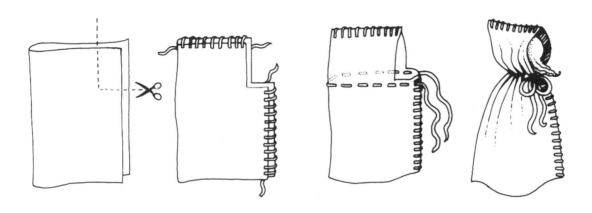

Picture Window Valentine

MATERIALS: Red construction paper, scissors, glue, white lacy paper doilies, photograph of the child's face, white crayon (sharp tipped), heart stickers

PROCEDURE: Fold construction paper in half and with a white crayon trace a half heart and two 1/2-inch lines from center fold with a 1-inch space between them. Children cut along these lines as carefully as possible, then open up heart and snip the fold between the two slits to create the window. Glue the child's photograph behind the window and glue the heart on a lacy paper doily. Print on the heart in white crayon: "Open the window and you will find someone who wants to be your Valentine!" Keep window closed with a heart sticker at the center fold until Valentines Day.

Valentine Crown

MATERIALS: Red felt (precut by adult with pinking shears into heart shape), white embroidery thread, large needles, gold elastic cord

PROCEDURE: Each child is given a red felt heart to sew a simple running stitch around edge (and inside, if so desired, but be sure stitches are loose to maintain heart shape). Adult measures child's head with gold cord and cuts appropriate length, sewing ends securely to either side of the felt heart. Children wear these crowns while doing the Valentine Dance:

Will you be my Valentine, my Valentine, my Valentine,
Will you be my Valentine and wear my big red heart?
Yes, I'll be your Valentine, your Valentine, your Valentine,
Yes, I'll be your Valentine and wear your big red heart!
Now we are sweet Valentines, sweet Valentines, sweet Valentines,
Now we are sweet Valentines, we wear our big red hearts!

Sing the above to the tune of "The Muffin Man." Divide children evenly into two circles, one inside the other. The inner circle remains in place, facing outward, while the outer circle skips around them in a clockwise direction, singing first two verses and stopping at the end of the verse in front of a child in the inner circle; they each gently touch the heart on the crown of this person. Then children on the inner circle skip in a clockwise direction singing the next two verses while the outer circle remains in place; they, too, stop at the end of their verse in front of a child and gently touch each other's heart crown. Now they hold hands together and skip in circle as partners, singing the last two verses. They can change places to repeat dance.

Winter Cooking and Baking

Fruit Cake

1 cup honey

2 cups warm water
  (approximately 110° F)

2 tablespoons yeast

3 cups whole wheat flour

3 cups unbleached white flour

1 teaspoon salt

1 tablespoon cinnamon

1 cup chopped dates

4 cups chopped apples

4 cups chopped nuts (walnuts,
  pecans, almonds, etc.)

1 tablespoon vanilla

1/2 cup oil

2 cups raisins

4 tablespoons orange rind

4 tablespoons lemon rind

In a large bowl, dissolve honey in warm water and gently stir in yeast; set aside to proof. Measure and mix dry ingredients (flours, salt, and cinnamon) in another bowl. Carefully supervise children if they help cut and chop the fruit and nuts. Add vanilla and oil to yeast mixture. Add dry ingredients to yeast mixture and mix thoroughly. Combine fruit and nuts, then fold into dough well. Divide mixture into three large greased loaf tins (or 6 small loaf tins for children to take home as gifts). Let rise for 2 hours. In preheated 350° F oven, bake for 1 hour (longer if testing knife comes out gooey). Cover with dish towel while cooling. Enjoy when cool, or wrap in plastic and freeze for later.

Gingerbread Men

2¾ cups sifted flour

3 teaspoons baking powder

½ teaspoon salt

2 teaspoons powdered ginger

⅔ cup molasses

¼ cup brown sugar

1 egg, well beaten

⅓ cup melted butter

Raisins

In a large bowl, sift together the first four dry ingredients. In another bowl, combine the next four ingredients and mix well. Add the wet ingredients to the dry ingredients and mix thoroughly. Roll out dough to desired thickness on a floured board with a floured rolling pin and cut with a floured cookie cutter, or let children mold their own gingerbread men (flattened to no less than ⅛ inch). Decorate with raisins for eyes, nose, etc. Bake on greased cookie sheet in preheated 350° F oven for 8 to 10 minutes (depending on thickness). Remove them from pan to cool. Makes about 1 dozen Gingerbread Men.

Honey Crispies

¼ cup butter

½ cup honey

2 cups sifted flour

¼ teaspoon salt

1 teaspoon baking soda

½ teaspoon cinnamon

¼ teaspoon allspice

¼ teaspoon nutmeg

¼ cup bran flakes or fine-ground granola

In a bowl, cream butter while slowly adding honey. In another bowl, sift together flour, salt, baking soda, and spices. Mix in bran flakes or granola to make crunchier cookies. Add these ingredients to butter mixture and stir well. Chill dough for at least 1 hour, until it is firm enough to roll to ⅛ inch on floured board. Cut with floured cookie cutters. Bake on greased cookie sheets in preheated 350° F oven for 10 to 12 minutes. Remove from baking sheet to cool. Makes about 3 dozen cookies.

Treasure Hide-Aways

1/2 cup butter
2/3 cup honey
2 eggs, beaten
1 1/2 teaspoons vanilla
3 1/2 cups whole wheat flour
2/3 teaspoon baking powder
1/2 tablespoon cinnamon

1/2 tablespoon nutmeg
Pinch of salt
1 cup chopped nuts (walnuts, pecans, almonds, etc.)
1 cup raisins or chopped fruit (apples, dates, etc.)

Cream the butter, honey, and eggs. Add vanilla. Combine flour with other dry ingredients. Add to the butter mixture. Form the dough into small balls with fingers or spoon; press down the center of a dough ball about halfway and fill with nuts and dried fruit treasure. Press dough over the hole to hide the treasure. Bake 10 to 12 minutes in a preheated 350° F oven on greased cookie sheets. Let cool before serving.

Walnut Molasses Bread

1/2 cup blackstrap molasses
1/2 cup brown sugar
2 tablespoons butter
2 cups whole wheat flour
1 teaspoon salt

3 teaspoons baking powder
1/2 cup white flour
1 cup milk
1 cup chopped walnuts

In a small bowl, cream together the first three ingredients. In a large bowl, sift together the four dry ingredients, then add milk and chopped walnuts. Combine all ingredients and mix well. Bake in a greased loaf pan for 1 hour in a preheated 350° F oven. Let cool before serving.

Granola Cookies

½ cup butter
½ cup honey
1½ teaspoons vanilla
1 egg
1 teaspoon salt
¾ teaspoon baking powder

½ cup whole wheat pastry flour
1 cup wheat germ
¾ cup oats
1 cup granola
Raisins (optional)

In a large bowl, cream together the first four ingredients. Mix the remaining ingredients together, then add to the creamed ingredients. Drop by rounded teaspoons onto a greased baking sheet. Bake in preheated 375° F oven for 10 to 12 minutes. Let cool before serving.

Eggnog

4 eggs
½ cup sugar
¼ teaspoon salt

4 cups cold milk
1 teaspoon vanilla
Nutmeg (optional)

Beat eggs, sugar, and salt with an electric or hand-held beater. Beat in the milk and vanilla. Sprinkle with nutmeg, if desired. Serve chilled.

Spiced Tea

Choose a favorite herb tea and brew as directed, or place a handful of dried herbs (peppermint or chamomile are good) in a preheated teapot. Pour boiling water over herbs and steep, covered, for 5 to 10 minutes. Add either a stick of cinnamon or a sprinkle of nutmeg to give it that final zip! For a wintry afternoon tea party, make spiced tea and a big batch of cookies. Or try a warm and toasty morning tea with toasted homemade bread and jam.

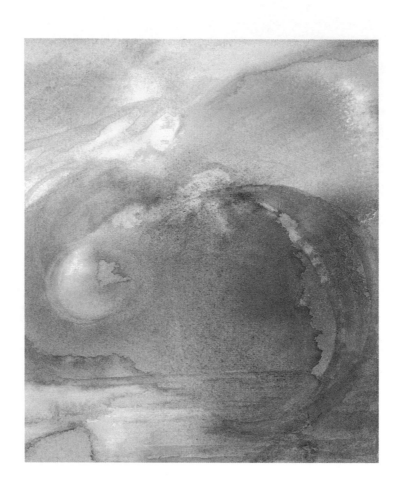

Spring

King Winter's crown becomes Lady Spring's garland. Life is budding and blooming from the earth, seeded and tended below by our elemental and insect friends. Above Father Sun, Sister Rain, Brother Wind, and our own helping hands do their part. Vegetable and flower beds that were prepared during the winter are awaiting the right moment for planting. In this chapter you will find circle games to enact Spring's promise with your children. Each seed child, sleeping in its being, is called softly to stretch and grow and glow in the light and warmth of the season. The animal kingdom is also abounding with new birth. Here are verses frisky with baby lambs and singing birds. Flower Fairies dance around dear Lady Spring.

The many rites of spring are given their rightful place imaginatively and according to cultural, religious, and seasonal heritage. In the symbols of spring festivals—the egg, the cross, the hare or rabbit—we see representations of transformation and new birth.

Now is a time to look at what is growing or needing to be planted in the garden of the young child's being. What are the child's individual and social needs? In this chapter you will find many projects and activities to nurture the young child's growth. Creating a small garden together, even if it's in a simple container, or taking walks to closely observe the natural sequence of plant growth from bud to blossom to fruit or vegetable can be a marvelous revelation. Such activities foster a sense of wonder, anticipation, and gratitude for life in children. Take your child's hand and step lightly into the beauty of spring-tide.

Spring Verses and Poems

Spring Is Coming

Traditional, words ∼ E. Jacobs, music

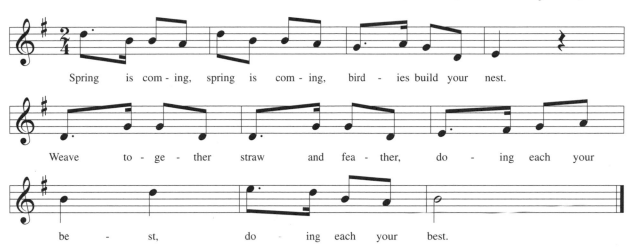

Spring is com - ing, spring is com - ing, bird - ies build your nest.

Weave to - ge - ther straw and fea - ther, do - ing each your

be - st, do - ing each your best.

2) Spring is coming, spring is coming,
   Flowers are waking too,
   Daisies, lilies, daffodillies,
   All are coming through,
   All are coming through.

3) Spring is coming, spring is coming,
   All around is fair,
   Shiver, quiver on the river,
   Joy is everywhere,
   Joy is everywhere!

Earth, Sun, Wind and Rain

Eileen Hutchins, words ∼ Peter Patterson, music

Mo - ther Earth, Mo - ther Earth. Take our seed and give it birth.

Fa - th - er Sun, Gle - am and glow, un - til the root be - g - ins to grow.

Sis - ter Rain, Si - s - ter Rain. Shed thy te - ars to swell the grain.

Br - o - ther Wind, bre - athe and blow, then the blade all gre - en will grow.

Earth and Sun and Wi - nd and Rain, Turn to gold the li - v - ing grain. (Hold voice) ... ...

(Lyre music at the end of each verse)

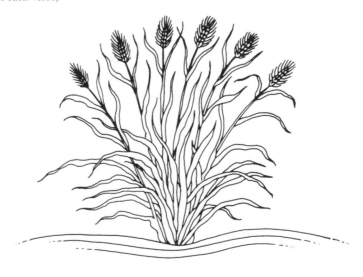

The Wind
Robert Louis Stevenson

I saw you toss the kites on high
And blow the birds about the sky;
And all around I heard you pass,
Like ladies skirts across the grass—
O wind, a-blowing all day long,
O wind that sings so loud a song!

I saw the different things you did,
But always you yourself you hid.
I felt you push, I heard you call,
I could not see yourself at all—
O wind a-blowing all day long,
O wind that sings so loud a song!

O you that are so strong and cold,
O blower, are you young or old?
Are you a beast of field and tree
Or just a stronger child than me?
O wind, a-blowing all day long,
O wind, that sings so loud a song!

The Shepherd's Sweet Lot
William Blake

How sweet is the shepherd's sweet lot!
From the morn to the evening he strays,
He shall follow his sheep all day,
And his tongue shall be filled with praise.
For he hears the lambs' innocent call,
And he hears the ewes' tender reply.
He is watchful while they are in peace,
For they know when the shepherd is nigh.

Silver Raindrops

Anonymous, words and music

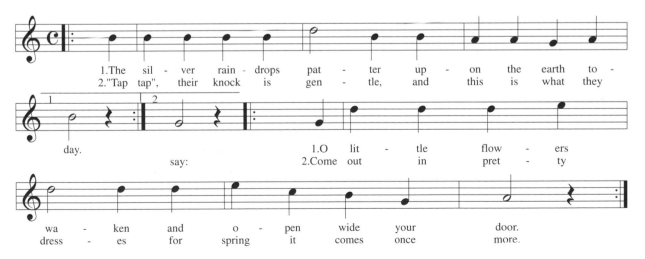

1.The sil - ver rain - drops pat - ter up - on the earth to -
2."Tap tap", their knock is gen - tle, and this is what they

day.
say:
1.O lit - tle flow - ers
2.Come out in pret - ty

wa - ken and o - pen wide your door.
dress - es for spring it comes once more.

Spring Is Singing
Betty Jones

Hear the birds sing their song
Now that spring has come along,
Hear each voice sweetly singing,
Joy and light to each heart bringing!
Robin Redbreast, Sparrow, Lark,
Thrush and Hummingbird listen—hark!
Other voices sing loud and clear,
It's the happy children—springtime's here!

Waterfall Fairies
Wendalyn von Meyenfeldt

Tinkle, tinkle, listen well,
Like a fairy's silver bell
In the distance ringing,
In the air, sweetly singing,
'Tis the water in the dell,
Where the elfin minstrels dwell,
Falling in a rainbow sprinkle,
Dropping stars that brightly twinkle,
On the sparkling pool below,
Making beautiful music so!
'Tis the little elves that play,
On their lutes of silver spray.
Tinkle, tinkle, fairy bell,
Like a pebble in a shell,
Tinkle, tinkle, listen well.

The Dream Fairy
Thomas Hood

A little fairy comes at night,
Her eyes are blue, her hair is brown,
With silver spots upon her wings,
And from the moon she flutters down.
She has a little silver wand,
And when a good child goes to bed,
She weaves her wee wand from right
   to left,
And makes a circle around their head.
And then it dreams of pleasant things,
Of fountains filled with fairy fish,
And trees that bear delicious fruit
And bow their branches at a wish,
Of arbors filled with dainty scents,
From lovely flowers that never fade,
Bright flies that glitter in the sun,
And glow-worms shining in the shade,
And talking birds with gifted tongues,
For singing songs and telling tales,
And pretty dwarfs to show the way,
Through fairy hills and fairy dales.

May Day

Good Morning, Mistress and Master,
I wish you a happy day;
Please to smell my garland
'Cause it's the First of May.

A branch of May I have brought you,
And at your door I stand;
It is but a sprout, but it's well budded out,
The work of Nature's hand.

Spring Movement and Creative Drama

Who Likes the Rain?
Clara Doty Bates

"I," said the duck, "I call it fun,
For I have my little red rubbers on!
They make a cunning three-toed track
In the soft cool mud. Quack! Quack! Quack!"

Duck-walk or waddle in a circle with bent knees and hands under arms while flapping arms like wings in rhythm.

"I," cried the dandelion, "I,
My roots are thirsty and my buds are dry!"
And she lifted a tousled yellow head,
Out of her green and grassy bed.

Cross arms, spread fingers and point down to represent roots. Lift head up and turn from side to side, stretching.

"I hope it will pour, I hope it will pour,"
Croaked the tree-toad at his grey backdoor.
"For with a broadleaf for a roof,
I'm perfectly weather-proof!"

Crouch and hop around.

Sang the brook, "I welcome every drop,
Come down dear raindrops; never stop
Until a broad river you make of me
And then I will carry you out to sea!"

Hold hands and tip-toe clockwise with tiny, rapid steps.

"I," shouted Ted, "for I can run
With my high-top boots and raincoat on,
Through every puddle and runlet and pool
I find on the road to school."

Run in place, put on imaginary boots and raincoats, then splash in a puddle.

Lady Spring

Anonymous, words ～ Margret Meyerkort, music

My La - dy Spring, she's dre - ssed in green, she wea - rs a prim - rose gown.
And lit - tle ba - by bu - ds and twigs are cl - ing - ing to her gown.

The sun shines if she laughs at all.
And if she weeps the rain - drops fall.

My La - dy Spring, My La - dy Spr - i - ng.

1st couplet: Children stand in a circle, holding each other's hands overhead. Lady Spring, wearing a flower crown, weaves in and out of circle during 1st couplet.

2nd couplet: Lady Spring stands in the center of the circle and, along with children, raises hands with

fingertips touching to make a circle overhead while turning in place one time. All children flutter fingers as raindrops.

3rd line: Lady Spring curtsies to the children and they bow to her. Change Lady Springs, and repeat. Boys love to be Lady Spring, too.

Growing Rhyme

J. M. Westrup

A farmer once planted some little brown
    seeds,

With a pit-a-pat, pit-a-pat, pit-a-pat,

He watered them often and pulled up the
    weeds,

With a tug-tug at this and a tug-tug at that,

The seeds they grew tall and green in the sun,

'Til a beautiful flower grew from each one,

With a hey-diddle

Holding their heads high in the air!

Crouch down; pretend to plant seeds.

Clap to beat of pit-a-pat.

*Make watering gesture, with thumb extended out
    from fist.*

Pull weeds to beat of tug-tug.

Grow tall from crouch; stretch arms up.

Wiggle fingers above head.

Dance around in a circle.

The Little Plant

Kate Louise Brown

In the heart of a seed buried deep so deep,	*Begin by crouching down in a circle.*
A dear little plant lay fast asleep.	*Make sleeping gesture with palms together.*
"Wake!" said the Sunshine, "And creep to the light!"	*Remain crouching, open eyes, look around surprised.*
"Wake!" said the voice of the raindrops bright.	*Remain crouching, put hand to ear.*
And the little plant heard and it rose to see,	*Rise slowly, stretch arms upward.*
What the wonderful outside world might be.	*Stand on tiptoes, turn in place.*

The Living Garden

Betty Jones

Little ants run to and fro, in and out the earth they go,
Busy, busy, never still, are the ants in their anthill.
Overhead the spider weaves its shining web among the trees,
And makes its thread so fine to snare unwary creatures, so beware!
Slowly, silently goes the snail, and leaves behind its gooey trail,
As it makes its slimy way whether it be night or day.
The buzzing bees sip here and there as fine flowers their nectar share,
Making honey, oh so sweet, those busy bees a working fleet.
Fuzzy caterpillar on this track, up and down goes his back
As he curls into a cocoon, who would guess that he'd be soon
The beautiful, winging butterfly, fluttering joyfully in the sky
And like a flower, her colors bright, fade into the darkest night.

In a circle, children act out the garden creatures as described. Ants scuttle around; spiders climb by inching hands upward with fingertips touching; snails slide slowly around the circle, bent over with their fists on their backs; bees quickly flutter their hands; caterpillars put their hands and feet on the floor, stretch out their bodies, and slowly inch their feet towards their hands; butterflies dance lightly in the circle.

Baby Seed Song

Edith Nesbit

Little brown brother, oh! little brown brother,
Are you awake in the dark?
Here we lie cozily, close to each other:
Hark to the sound of the lark—
"Waken!" the lark says, "Waken and dress
    you;
Put on your green coats and gay,
Blue sky will shine on you, sunshine caress
    you,
Waken! 'tis morning—'tis May!"

Little brown brother, oh! little brown brother,
What kind of flower will you be?
I'll be a poppy—all white, like my mother;
Do be a poppy like me.
What! you're a sunflower? How I shall
    miss you
When you've grown golden and high!
But I shall send all the bees up to kiss you;
Little brown brother, good-bye.

Begin by standing in a circle; slowly bend down and curl up on the floor as if sleeping.

Put hand to ear in a listening gesture.

Flap wings and rise up.

Throw open arms overhead and turn once in place.

Crouch, cup hands, and look inside them.

Pop up with feet and arms spread wide.

Jump feet together; clap hands overhead.

Flutter fingers and make buzzing sound.
End by blowing kiss and waving goodbye.

Lambs

Christina Rossetti

On the grassy banks,
Lambkins at their pranks,
Wooly sisters, wooly brothers,
Jumping off their feet,
While their wooly mothers,
Watch by them and bleat!

Children can choose to be lambkins, jumping and playing in the center of a circle, or mother lambs, bleating at the periphery of the circle while beckoning lambkins to come rest near them. One by one, each lambkin chooses a mother in the circle to go to. Repeat verse until all lambkins have finished playing and have gone to stand by a mother.

Little White Lily

George MacDonald

Little White Lily sat by a stone,
Drooping and waiting 'til the sun shone.
Little White Lily, sunshine was fed,
Little White Lily is lifting her head.
Little White Lily said, "It's good,
Little White Lily's clothing and food."
Little White Lily dressed like a bride,
Shining with brightness and crowned beside.
Little White Lily, drooping with pain,
Waiting and waiting for the wet rain.
Little White Lily, holdeth her cup,
Rain is fast falling and filling it up.
Little White Lily said, "Good again,
Now I am stronger. Now I am cool.
Heat cannot burn me, my veins are so full!"
Little White Lily smells very sweet,
On her head sunshine, rain at her feet.
Thanks to the sunshine, thanks to the rain,
Little White Lily is happy again.

Begin by sitting in a circle; all children act out Little White Lily. Let them improvise based on the verse.

Pussy Willow

I know a pussy willow,
Her fur is pearly grey,
She lives down in the meadow,
Not very far away,
She'll always be a pussy,
She'll never be a cat,
For she's a pussy willow,
Now what do you think of that?
Meow-meow-meow-meow-meow-meow-
　　meow-SCAT!

Sing each line of poem proceeding upward from Middle C of the musical scale, one note per line; allow your hand to follow notes upward from your lap to above your head, then proceed down the scale with each "Meow," and at the last, clap hands loudly at SCAT!

May Song

Betty Jones

Sing a song of May Day—Hi-dee-ho-dee-hey!
Showers of flowers from breezy bowers—Hi-dee-ho-dee-hey!
Dancers and prancers in the high grass—Hi-dee-ho-dee-hey!
Joyfully skip each young lad and lass—Hi-dee-ho-dee-hey!
Happy, oh happy May Day, May Day!
Happy, oh happy May Day—hey!

This verse lends itself to a simple tune like "Sing a Song of Six Pence" or one spontaneously created with the children. The words may be spoken and the "Hi-dee-ho-dee-hey!" part may be sung. See Spring Art and Handwork for instructions on making a Simple Maypole and May Day Crowns. As for dancing 'round the Maypole, each child holds a ribbon from the Maypole; a maximum of 8 can do this at any one time. Be sure Maypole is secure. Wearing May Day crowns, children dance or skip in rhythm, clockwise, around Maypole while singing. Then, unwind ribbon by reversing direction. Each child may have a partner to hold hands with. One child holds the ribbon while the other skips alongside. If this is done, have the children take turns holding the ribbon. Be sure to emphasize the need to hold the ribbon high up, so that the Maypole, not the children, becomes wrapped in ribbon!

Bunny and the Garden

Betty Jones

*Begin by sitting in a circle; all children
act like the bunny.*

A bunny sits with pricked up ears,	*Raise both hands behind head as ears.*
Listens well before he dares	*Make listening gesture at one ear, then the other.*
To hop, hop, hop from his bunny hole	*Hop around in place.*
To the farmer's garden where the carrots grow	*Stop hopping.*
To pick and nibble those crunchy delights	*Make eating gesture.*
From the cabbage too, he takes a few bites.	*Hop a bit, then pick and eat more.*
With his tummy full, he washes his face	*Pat tummy; put hands to face in washing gesture.*
'Til the farmer yells and begins the chase!	*Raise hands and place behind head as ears.*
With a hippity-hop-hop and a leaping bound,	*Hop hurriedly near place in circle.*
Bunny hides safely in his hole in the ground.	*Return to place in circle; hide by covering head.*

The Clocking Hen

"Will you take a walk with me,
Clocking hen, today?
There's barley in the barley fields
And hayseed in the hay."
"Thank you," said the clocking hen,
"I've something else to do;
I'm busy sitting on my eggs,
I cannot walk with you."
"Clock, clock, clock, clock,"
Said the clocking hen;
"My little chicks will soon be hatched,
I'll think about it then."
The clocking hen sat on her nest
She made it in the hay;
And warm and snug beneath her breast
A dozen white eggs lay.
Crack, crack, went all the eggs;
Out dropped the chickens small!
"Clock, clock," said the clocking hen,
"Now I have you all!
Come along my little chicks,
I'll take a walk with you. "
"Hallo!" said the barnyard cock,
"Cock-a-doodle-doo!"

*Children can act out all characters in this barnyard
scene. Begin by walking in a circle like Rooster with
exaggerated high steps, arms bent at elbows and
tucked under arms like wings. Continue to flap
wings but stop and slowly sit down on imaginary
eggs, while saying the Mother Hen verses. At "crack,
crack," tap fingertips of cupped hands together, and
then wiggle fingers as chicks. At "clock, clock," get
up and walk in circle with wings fluttering, until
"Hallo." End by stopping and standing on one leg
at "Cock-a-doodle-doo!"*

Ducks
Betty Jones

"Quack, quack, quack," through reeds
    and muck,
Paddle, waddle, here come the ducks!
Heads bob up and tails wig-wag,
Mom leads the way while babes play tag!
Splashing, dashing in the water,
"Quack, quack, quack!" away ducks
    totter!

*Model duck-walk by tucking hands under arms
for wings, stooping low, bobbing head, and
wiggling hind-end in place. In a circle, children
duck-walk, and waddle around circle, increasing
their speed at the word "tag." At "splashing,"
flutter wings and hop in toward center of circle;
continue to waddle around this smaller circle,
flapping wings. Be sure everyone joins in with
"Quack, quack, quack!"*

Rainbow Fairies

Two little clouds one spring day,
Went flying through the sky;
They went so fast they bumped their heads,
And both began to cry.
Old Father Sun came out and said:
"Oh, never mind my dears,
I'll send my little fairy folk
To dry your falling tears."
One fairy came in violet, and one in indigo;
In blue, green, yellow, orange and red,
They made a pretty row.
They wiped the cloud tears all away
And then from out the sky,
Upon a line a sunbeam made,
They hung their gowns to dry.

*Begin in a circle with children acting out all parts.
Fly, waving arms while moving in one direction;
bump head with fist and make crying gesture.
Make large circle with arms around head, fingertips
touching, for Father Sun. End as fairies: hop up
and flutter wings, wipe away tears, and reach high
on tip-toes to hang gowns out to dry on imaginary
sunbeam.*

The Little Men
Flora Fearne

Would you see the Little Men
Coming down a moon-lit glen?
Gnome and elf and woodland sprite,
Clad in brown and green and white,
Skipping, hopping, never stopping,
Stumbling, grumbling, tumbling,
    mumbling,
Dancing, prancing, singing, swinging—
Coats of red and coats of brown,
Put on straight or upside down,
Outside in and inside out,
Some with sleeves and some without,
Rustling, bustling, stomping, romping,
Strumming, humming, hear them coming—
You will see the Little Men
If it be a fairy glen.

*Children move in one direction around a circle to
the rhythm of the verse (skipping, hopping, etc.).
Stop in place and pretend to dress self. Continue
described movements in verse, encouraging all
Little Men to improvise to words and rhythm.*

Fairy Ring

Round about, round about, in a fairy ring,
Thus we dance, thus we dance, and thus
    we sing!
Trip and go, to and fro, over this green grass
    we go,
All about, in and out, for our Flower Queen!

*Children skip or dance in a circle; improvise a tune to
accompany the words, and also improvise movements
like holding hands while moving in and out of circle.
End by bowing to a Flower Queen in the center.*

Fairy Music Makers
Betty Jones

Fairy Music Makers, oh!
From Fairyland we come to show
How to make sweet music so
Would you like to hear?
A-ring-a-ring-a-ring-oh!
A-zing-a-zing-a-zing, high-low,
The violin so fine does go
Resounding far and near... hear!
A-ting-a-ling-a-ling-oh!
Our triangles like to sing so
Swing merrily to and fro, oh!
Here in Fairyland.

Rum-a-tum-a-tum-oh!
So the Fairyland drums go
Calling each fairy, hey-hey-ho!
Come and play with us today!

Children skip around in a circle in one direction. At "Would you like to hear?" all stop and take a violin stance and pretend to fiddle. Then make triangle with index finger and thumb of one hand spread wide while other index finger rings by tapping them. End by marching in original direction, beating imaginary drum in rhythm to the words.

Spring Fingerplays and Riddles

My Garden
Betty Jones

This is my wee garden plot,
I'll rake it with care and it will grow a lot!
Peas and carrots and salad from seeds,
I'll plant and water and pull out the weeds.
The sun will shine and bathe my garden
   in light,
All the plants will be happy and taste
   just right!
Here, try some, have a bite!

Extend palm, point to it with index finger of other hand.
Make rake with spread fingers and stroke it over palm.
Poke index finger around palm to plant seeds.
Extend thumb from fist to pour; pinch palm to weed.
Flex and contract fingers.

Face palms up and wiggle fingers.

Extend garden palm outward, pick plant, pop into mouth, and chew.

Little Brown Seed

Rodney Bennet

Little seed, round and sound,	*Make "O" with fingers.*
Here I put you in the ground.	*Place "seed" in palm of other hand.*
You can sleep a week or two,	*Make sleeping gesture with hands to head.*
Then I'll tell you what to do!	*Point thumb at self, shake index finger in rhythm.*
You must grow some downward roots,	*Point index fingers down.*
Then some tiny, upward shoots.	*Point index fingers up.*
From these roots folded sheaves,	*Cup hands tightly together.*
Soon must come some healthy leaves.	*Unfurl cupped hands.*
When the leaves have time to grow,	*Spread hands widely.*
Next a bunch of buds must show.	*Make "O"s with fingers.*
Last of all the buds must spread,	*Open "O"s into widely cupped hands.*
Into blossoms white and red.	*Wiggle fingers.*
There seed, now, I've done my best,	*Point to self.*
Please to grow and do the rest!	*Cross arms over chest and nod "yes."*

Five Little Peas

Five little peas in a pea pod pressed,	*Begin sitting in a circle with fists clenched.*
One grew, two grew, so did all the rest.	*Raise one finger at a time.*
They grew and they grew and they did not stop,	*Gradually raise hand over head; open and close fist.*
Until one day, the pod went POP!	*Clap hands overhead. Repeat with other hand.*

The Egg

Within marble walls as white as milk,
Lined with a skin as soft as silk,
No doors are there to this stronghold,
Yet thieves break in and steal the gold.

Little Brown Rabbit

A little brown rabbit popped out of the ground,	*Right index and middle fingers pop up.*
Wriggled his whiskers and looked all around.	*Wiggle rabbit-ear fingers.*
Another wee rabbit who lived in the grass,	*Left rabbit ears pop up.*
Popped his head out and watched him pass.	*Right hand crosses over left hand at wrists.*
Then both wee rabbits went hippity-hop-hippity-hop-hippity-hop,	*Hop both hands.*
'Til they came to a wall and had to stop.	*Both hands stop suddenly.*
Then both wee rabbits turned themselves around,	*Uncross hands.*
And scuttled off home to their holes in the ground.	*Hands hop back to sides and hide behind back.*

To Let

D. Newey-Johnson

Two little beaks went tap, tap, tap!	*Cup hands; tap index fingers together.*
Two little shells went crack, crack, crack!	*Cup hands; tap all fingertips three times.*
Two fluffy chicks peeped out and Oh!	*Stop tapping; swivel hands to look around.*
They liked the looks of the big world so,	*Open hands wide; spread arms out.*
They left their homes without a fret,	*Put hands behind back.*
And two little shells are now to let!	*Bring cupped hands in front.*

Bluebird

Betty Jones

Begin with one hand out flat with other fist on top as bluebird.

Bluey, bluey bluebird sits in a tree	*Thumb protrudes as bluebird.*
Bluey, bluey bluebird nods at me.	*Nod thumb.*
Bluey, bluey bluebird chirps, "Good day."	*Tap thumb and index finger together to chirp.*
Spreads his wings and flies away!	*Clasp thumbs and wave fingers to "fly away."*

Mama Bird, Have You Heard?

Betty Jones

Let children guess word in parentheses. Extend fingers
of one hand for tree, cup fingers of other hand as nest.

In the branches of a tree a little _____
   (nest)

Place nest between thumb and index finger
   branches.

Mama Bird will take her rest

Wiggle thumb of nest-hand for Mama Bird.

And sit and wait for her _____ (eggs) to hatch

Hold still, then wiggle fingers as babies hatch.

Then for her babies wiggly _____ (worms)
   to catch!

Wiggle index finger of other hand as worm;
   nest-hand becomes beak and eats worm.

'Til the day they fly from the _____ (nest)

"Fly" fingers of nest-hand behind back.

Good Mama Bird will do her best!

Wiggle thumb from empty branch for Good
   Mama Bird.

Finger Fairies

Betty Jones

Fairies funny, five are we,

Laughing, happy as can be

Dance hand back and forth.

HA-HA-HA

Wiggle thumb.

HEE-HEE-HEE

Wiggle index finger.

HO-HO-HO

Wiggle middle finger.

WEE-WEE-WEE

Wiggle ring finger.

And away we go!

Wiggle pinkie and fly away fingers behind back.

Repeat verse using other hand.

Bunny Riddle

Guess who hops wherever he goes?
Wiggle, wiggle, goes his nose.
His ears are pink, his tail is funny.
Can you guess, it's a _____!

Wind

You can never really see me
But you see the things I do,
In March I make many breezes
To fly your kite for you!
What is my name?

Spring Games

Five Tiny Fairies

Five tiny fairies hiding in a flower.
Five tiny fairies caught in a shower.
Daddy Cock-a-doodle standing on one leg.
Old Mother Speckle-top lays a golden egg.
Old Mrs. Crosspatch comes with a stick,
Fly away fairies, quick, quick, quick!

*Choose one child to be Mrs. Crosspatch; she
hides outside circle. Children stand in circle. Five
fairy children crouch in center of circle with arms
folded over heads. Children in outer circle flutter
fingers with swaying arms held up, making rain.
Fairy children continue to crouch. Circle children
stand on one leg with hands under arms making
wings. Sit down with wings flapping and remain
seated still flapping wings. Mrs. Crosspatch comes
holding up an imaginary stick and enters circle.
Seated children yell, "Fly away fairies quick, quick,
quick!" and clap hands three times. Fairy children
jump up and run to the arms of a child in the circle.
The five befriending children become the next fairies,
Mrs. Crosspatch chooses a replacement, and the
game begins again.*

Five Little Seeds

Five little seeds a-sleeping they lay,
A-sleeping they lay,
A bird flew down and took one away;
How many seeds were left?
Four little seeds a-sleeping they lay,
etc.…

*Five children curl up on the floor; the child who
is the bird stands on a footstool with arms outstretched, jumps down, and "flies" one seed child
away; when all the seeds have been taken, the
rest of the group blow all the seeds back again.*

Spring Art and Handwork

Pom-pom Animals

MATERIALS: Stiff card or poster board, scissors, various colors of wool yarn, large blunt needle

PROCEDURE: Cut two 2-inch circles from stiff card or poster board. Cut a 1/2-inch doughnut hole in each. Place the two circles together. Wind wool continuously around outside and through the center hole (spacing evenly), until the center is completely filled. When it becomes difficult to get the wool through the center by hand, thread the yarn through a large needle and proceed until doughnut hole is well filled. With sharp scissors, cut around the outer edge between the two circles. Then attach a heavy thread or strong yarn between the two circles, tying very tightly. Remove the circles and fluff the yarn pom-pom. Use as the head for an animal. Repeat the process for the body by cutting two 4-inch circles with 1-inch doughnut holes and proceeding as before. Attach this pom-pom to the head by tying securing threads together. Trim the fuzzy animal (chick, duck, bunny, lamb, kitten, etc.). Sew on colored felt for beaks, ears, tails, etc., and embroider eyes if desired. Vary circle sizes for more variety.

Caterpillar

MATERIALS: Paper egg cartons cut into 3- or 4-cup sections, paint, brushes, pipe cleaners, colored paper, scissors, glue

PROCEDURE: Paint the cup sections and allow to dry. Cut a strip of colored paper the same length as that of the cup sections and at least 1/2 inch wider on each side. Snip along these wider edges, making feet. Glue the painted section to this strip, cup side up. Bend pipe cleaner to "V" shape and glue to the forehead of the caterpillar as antennae. Paint or glue paper pieces for the eyes.

Butterflies

MATERIALS: Black and white construction paper and 2 sheets wax paper (all with the same dimensions), several different colored wax crayons, grater, scissors, iron, tea towel

PROCEDURE: Fold black and white papers in half. Trace half a butterfly shape on the folded white paper with half butterfly body on the fold. Cut around outline, making a pattern for the black paper. Align folds and trace pattern onto black paper. Cut as before. Now you have two butterfly shapes and two frames from which they have been cut. With adult supervision, children grate different colored wax crayons on one sheet of wax paper. Spread the shavings. Cover with another wax sheet. Place the wax sheets between folds of a tea towel. An adult should press with a hot iron to melt the crayons. Glue or staple this piece between the black and white frame pieces. Hang in the window to let the sun shine through this colored butterfly! You can then paint (with a wet-on-wet watercolor technique, or "drop and splatter" tempera paints) or color the black and white butterfly centers and hang them with string to fly.

Helping Hands Card

MATERIALS: Colored construction paper, white poster or tempera paint in tray, crayons

PROCEDURE: This card is perfect for Mothers' or Fathers' Day. Fold construction paper in half. Open it. Have the child dip whole hand flat (first right, then left) into tray of white paint and press hand on each half of paper. Let dry. Wash hands. Cut pieces of white paper to glue to inside of card and let children draw their own picture of what they would like to do for Mother or Father with their helping hands. On the inside of the card, this verse could be printed:

These are my hands, Dear Mother (Father),
They are just for you today,
I'll show you how much I love you
By helping in every way!

May Day Crowns

MATERIALS: Cut branches, strong thread, flowers, ribbons of various colors and lengths

PROCEDURE: Go on a May Day walk and carefully cut (with permission!) assorted flowers and long flexible branches with foliage. Tie the branch to fit the head of the child. With the thread attached, let the child wind it around the foliage, attaching cut flowers at intervals. Decorate with pastel-colored ribbons that fly as child dances.

Simple Maypole

MATERIALS: Thick wooden dowel (1½-inch diameter, 9 feet long), 8 variously colored ribbons (1 inch wide, 12 feet long), tacks

PROCEDURE: Securely tack ribbons to top of dowel, evenly spaced around dowel's circumference. Maypole can be held on a Christmas tree stand filled with heavy stones or, alternatively, secure firmly in earth so that children cannot dislodge it. Maypole should extend to at least 4 feet above children's heads.

Tiny Turtle

MATERIALS: Small piece of cardboard, pencil, scissors, glue, walnut shell half, colored paper

PROCEDURE: Using the walnut shell as a guide for size, trace a small turtle shape onto colored paper. Cut this shape and glue it to the piece of cardboard, then cut the cardboard. Bend the neck up and the head down. Bend the feet up and the legs down (dotted lines in illustration show where to fold the cardboard). Glue the bottom of the walnut shell edge and center it on the back of the turtle.

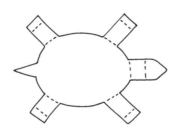 

Spring Cooking and Baking

Hot Cross Buns

A traditional Eastertime treat. Let young chefs measure and count out the milk (1 cup equals 16 tablespoons).

4 cups unbleached white flour	1 ounce yeast
	1 cup warm milk (110° F)
1 tablespoon salt	1/4 cup butter
1/2 tablespoon allspice	1 egg, beaten
1/2 tablespoon nutmeg	1/2 cup currants
1/2 tablespoon cinnamon	2 tablespoons orange peel
1/4 cup raw sugar	

Glaze

2 tablespoons sugar	2 tablespoons water

In a large bowl, thoroughly combine flour, salt, and spices. In a separate bowl, dissolve sugar and yeast in warm milk and let proof. Cut butter into dry ingredients; add yeast mixture, egg, currants, and peel. Knead well. Cover and put dough in warm place to rise to double its size. Divide dough into 12 to 16 parts for children to knead on floured surface. Shape into buns. Place buns on greased baking sheets. Let rise until doubled. With knife, slash a cross on top of each bun before baking in preheated 450° F oven for 15 to 20 minutes. To make the glaze, combine sugar and water. Bring to a boil, stirring to prevent burning; let cool. Glaze buns when buns and glaze are cool.

Coconut Easter Eggs

2 1/2 cups confectioners' sugar	1/4 tablespoon vanilla
1 3-ounce package of cream cheese, softened	Dash of salt
	Grated coconut

Cream sugar and cream cheese until smooth. Beat in vanilla and salt. Cover and refrigerate for 1 hour. Shape dough into small balls and roll in coconut. Place "eggs" on wax paper–lined cookie sheets and refrigerate for 1 hour.

Easter Bunny Fruit Salad

Pear halves
Lettuce leaves
Raisins

Red apples
Cottage cheese

Place pear half on top of the lettuce leaf with the narrow end as the head of the bunny. Eyes are two raisins and nose is a chunk of apple. Ears are made from the apple cut lengthwise (approximately ⅛ apple slice). A ball of cottage cheese is bunny's tail!

Cupcakes

2¼ cups pastry flour
3 teaspoons baking powder
1 tablespoon cinnamon
1 teaspoon salt
1 cup honey

½ cup oil
½ cup milk
2 eggs
2 teaspoons vanilla

Carob Frosting

¼ cup butter
1½ cups milk powder
½ cup carob powder

½ cup honey
½ cup milk
2 teaspoons vanilla

In a large bowl, combine dry ingredients. In a separate bowl, mix together wet ingredients. Combine wet and dry ingredients; mix well. Fill cupcake cups ½ to ¾ full. Bake in preheated 350° F oven for 30 to 35 minutes. Makes 15 to 18 cupcakes. To make frosting, cream together the butter and milk powder. Add the carob powder and beat well. Add the honey, milk, and vanilla, and beat until smooth. Let cupcakes cool before frosting.

A Child's Seasonal Treasury

Summer

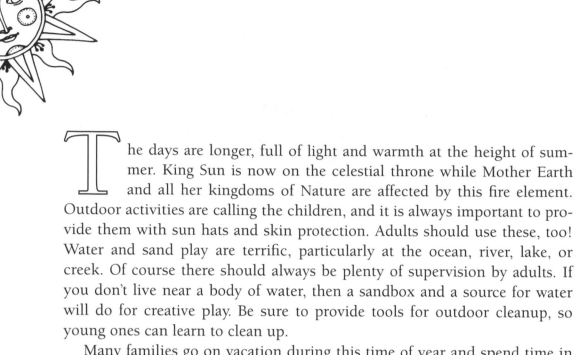

The days are longer, full of light and warmth at the height of summer. King Sun is now on the celestial throne while Mother Earth and all her kingdoms of Nature are affected by this fire element. Outdoor activities are calling the children, and it is always important to provide them with sun hats and skin protection. Adults should use these, too! Water and sand play are terrific, particularly at the ocean, river, lake, or creek. Of course there should always be plenty of supervision by adults. If you don't live near a body of water, then a sandbox and a source for water will do for creative play. Be sure to provide tools for outdoor cleanup, so young ones can learn to clean up.

Many families go on vacation during this time of year and spend time in Nature, camping and absorbing the sensory experiences of clean air, fresh sparkling waters, colorful stones and plants, and different landscapes and animals. This chapter presents verses, activities, and games for romping under bright King Sun during the summer-tide.

Summer Verses and Poems

Daisies and Grasses

Daisies so bright, grasses so green,
Tell me I pray, how do you keep clean?
Summertime showers, summertime rain,
Wash dusty flowers all clean again.

Babbling Brook

Betty Jones

Babbling Brook bubbles and runs
Along its merry way,
Tumbles o'er rocks, through reeds,
Babbling Brook, what have you to say?
"Curly, furly, fresh young ferns
Shade my waters clear,
Freckled fish flit beneath me,
Birds sing and bring good cheer!
All the joys of summer
As I run along,
I love to be a Babbling Brook
And share my water song!"

The Tree

Björnstjerne Björnson

The tree's early leaf buds were bursting
    their brown:
"Shall I take them away?" said the frost,
    sweeping down.
"No, dear; leave them alone,
Till blossoms here have grown,"
Prayed the tree, while it trembled from
    root to crown.

The tree bore its blossoms, and all the
    birds sung.
"Shall I take them away?"
Said the wind, as it swung.
"No, dear; leave them alone
Till berries here have grown,"
Said the tree, while its leaflets quivering
    hung.

The tree bore its fruit in the midsummer
    glow:
Said the girl, "May I gather thy berries
    or no?"
"Yes, dear, all thou canst see;
Take them; all are for thee,"
Said the tree, while it bent its laden
    boughs low.

The Midsummer Garden

Eileen Hutchins, words ~ Peter Patterson, music

We si - ng you a - sto - ry, a wo - n - der - ful sto - ry, we

si - ng you a - sto - ry of Mi - d sum - mer Night. We

sing you th - e song of th - e da - nce o - f th - e fai - ries. We

sing you th - e song of th - e ro - se bu - d o - f light.

2) We gather the blossom, the snow white blossom, the rose red blossom to twine in our hair.
We sip of the honey, the golden honey, we sip of the honey so sweet and rare.

3) We go to the fountain, the sparkling fountain, we go to the fountain for water fair.
The wind on the fountain, the sparkling fountain, has stirred the water that floweth fair.

4) We taste of the water, the sparkling water, the living water that floweth fair.
And there in the twilight the fairies are dancing, the fairies are dancing as light as air.

5) They lead to the garden, the midsummer garden, they lead to the garden where roses bloom.
The flowers are singing, are swaying and singing, the flowers are singing with stars and with moon.

6) And there is the Mother, the white-robed Mother, the Mother of all who shines in light.
She gives us a rose from her garland of roses, she gives us a rosebud so pure and white.

7) Oh, guard it forever the beautiful blossom, oh, guard it forever the rose of light.

Bubbles

Betty Jones

Bubbles are a lovely thing to blow
On a hot, dry summer day,
Big and small, they rise and fall
And POP! along the way.
Sparkling crystal rainbows
In the sunshine bright,
How I'd love to be a bubble
And sail into the night.

Foxglove

Betty Jones

Foxglove, foxglove, growing up so tall,
What do you see o'er the garden wall?
Bumblebees and hummingbirds sipping
    from each flower,
Caterpillars and slimy snails inching by
    the hour,
Gurgling brook and croaking frog sing a
    tender song,
And children skipping down the path of
    summer days so long!

Summer
Movement and Creative Drama

My Horses

My white horses like to step
Peaceful and slow,
Over mountains, through valleys,
So upright they go.
My brown horses merrily
Trot in the sun,
With their silver hooves beating
The ground as they run.

My black horses gallop
With courage around,
And they throw up their heads
As they hammer the ground.

*Children enact horse movements as described,
moving in one direction around a circle.*

Fishermen

Betty Jones

Begin by standing in a circle.

Heave-ho! your nets to throw,	*Twist, fling arms out; twist back, fling arms in.*
Fishermen, what will you catch?	*Pull nets in hand over hand.*
Waves will roll, winds will call,	*Make rolling arm movements toward inner circle.*
Fishermen, you've met your match!	*Make larger rolling arm movements.*
Pull-tug, your nets like a rug,	*Pull on nets hard toward self.*
Fishermen, make your wish.	*Make prayer gesture at heart level.*
Slip, slide, what can be inside?	*Slide feet sideways; peer toward center.*
Fishermen, you've caught lots of fish!	*Pretend to hold slippery fish; dance for joy.*

Creature Features

Betty Jones

Slinking, creeping, Kitty-cat sly,
Watches the birds go fluttering by,
To pounce and catch one Kitty will try!
Hoppity-poppity from his hole in the ground,
Bunny jumps and leaps without a sound,
'Til he stops to nibble greens he's found.
Slowly, carefully, trods the tortoise old,
Carrying his house on his back so bold,
It guards him from harsh sun and cold.

Standing in a circle, children imitate slinking and pouncing kitty-cat; pop up from crouched position and hop as a bunny, then stop to "nibble"; lastly, put arms behind back and stoop over while moving slowly as a tortoise.

Beehive

Emily Poullson

Here is the beehive, where are the bees?	*Hold out clenched fist.*
Hidden away where nobody sees!	*Look at fist; shake head "no."*
Here they come creeping out of the hive,	*Open fist slowly, gradually extend fingers.*
One, two, three, four, five,	
ZOOM, ZOOM, ZOOM, see they're alive!	*Flutter fingers all around in rhythm.*

Little Fish

I saw a little fish come swimming past,
And I said, "Little Fish why do you go
  so fast?
Can't you stop a moment and play
  with me?"
But he wagged his little tail and swam down
  to the sea.

Beginning in a circle, children make a breast stroke swimming gesture while walking in one direction, moving faster during second line. All stop, hold hands and bow toward center, drop hands, and "swim" in same direction as before.

Little Birdie

I saw a little birdie coming hop, hop, hop!
And I said, "Little Birdie, won't you stop,
  stop, stop?
Won't you stop a moment and play
  with me?"
But he wagged his little tail and away
  flew he!

Beginning in a circle, children hold their hands under their armpits like wings, look left, then right, and hop toward center three times at "hop, hop, hop." At second line, all stop, look left, then right, hop three times toward center at "stop, stop, stop." All hold hands, bow toward center. End by dropping hands, make "wings" again and "fly" back to the periphery.

Big Cow

I saw a big cow saying, "Moo, moo, moo,"
And I said, "Big, big cow, how do you do,
  do, do?
Can't you come awhile and play with
  me?"
"I'm busy eating grass to make milk for
  your tea!"

Beginning in a circle on hands and knees, children move toward the center with slow deliberate gait, stop and look at each other while saying, "Moo, moo, moo." Continue toward center in same manner for next two lines. On the last line, all bend heads down and pretend to eat grass.

White Horses

Irene F. Pawsey

Far out at sea there are horses to ride,
Little white horses that race with the tide,
Their tossing manes are the white sea
  foam,
And the lashing winds are driving them
  home,
To shadowy stables, fast they must flee,
To the great green caravan under the sea.

Children pretend to mount their seahorses, then trot and gallop going in one direction around a circle. Shake heads and return to original place in circle. Repeat going opposite direction.

The Fairy Ball

Betty Jones

In the East the Sunshine Castle sparkled
    with golden light,
A Fairy Ball for one and all was scheduled
    for that night.
The Fairy folk cleaned the hall and dressed
    all to a "T,"
Suits and dresses, curling tresses, from the
    biggest to the most tiny.
But one little Fairy, Chloe, in a rosebud,
    took a rest,
While her Fairy sisters and brothers
    prepared for each guest.

The clock struck nine, the party began,
    and the Fairy folk danced through
    the door,
The rosebud opened for a look at the fun
    and Chloe fell—Plop!—on the floor!
"Oh, my! Oh, my!" she began to cry, "I'm
    not ready for the ball!"
But from a Wise One's wink, Chloe
    changed in a blink to the fairest Fairy
    of all!

*Improvise this fairy ball with Chloe and rosebud
in the center of a circle and all the fairy folk
around them enacting out the verses.*

Sunshine Fairies

Betty Jones

We are the sunshine fairies
And with our sparks of light,
We shimmer and glimmer in the air,
Hugging flowers with colors bright!

*Begin standing in a circle; children hold out their
arms at their sides and turn in place clockwise as
fairies. Stop, and flick fingers as sparks. Hold out
arms at sides, flutter fingers, then turn in place
counterclockwise; hug self and rub hands up and
down over folded arms.*

The Giant

Betty Jones

Giant I am and giant I'll be, Striding o'er mountains, Striding o'er sea. A fee-hee, fi-hi, fo-ho, fum! Watch out world, here I come!	*Children take giant steps around a circle, puffing out their chests and swinging their arms until "here I come." End by stopping, turning in place, and giant-stepping in opposite direction. Repeat verse and actions.*

Flower Elves

Pretty flower elves are we, Dancing to and fro, Peeping out from neath our buds As round and round we go.	*Children skip around a circle with colored veils.*
Sleepy, sleepy snails are we Our steps are long and slow. We drag our feet along the ground As round and round we go.	*Children take big slow steps around a circle.*
Butterflies from the air are we Our wings are fairy light. We dance before the king and queen Upon the flowers bright.	*Children skip around a circle while flapping their arms.*
Funny little gnomes are we, Our beards are long and white, Towards the rocks our footsteps turn To tap from morn 'til night.	*Children trudge, bent over, around a circle while hammering fist on fist.*
A long green snake in the grass are we Our tail is far away. We wriggle and wriggle and twist and turn As in and out we sway.	*Children put together outstretched arms and hands and act out described movements while walking around a circle.*

Summer Fingerplays and Riddles

Fish Alive

One, two, three, four, five,
Once I caught a fish alive!
Six, seven, eight, nine, ten,
Then I let it go again!
Why did I let it go?
Because it bit my finger so!
Which finger did it bite?
This finger on the right.

Make a fist and unfurl fingers one at a time.
Wiggle all five fingers.
Bow a finger for each number spoken.
Wiggle fingers; hide hand behind back.
Shrug sholders.
Point right index finger and nip it.
Close fist.
Hold up right index finger and wiggle it.

My Turtle

Betty Jones

Here is my turtle's shell.
Knock! Knock! Knock! Anyone home?
Slowly, carefully, he pokes out his head
And on his four legs he begins to roam
'Til the night comes, then it's time for bed.
My turtle tucks in his own legs and head.

Make fist.
Knock on shell with other fist.
Extend thumb from shell fist.
*Extend four bent shell fingers and creep along
    other outstretched arm.*
Stop; curl fingers and thumb back into fist.

Dandelion

Betty Jones

Dandelion so white and furry,
When summer breezes blow
You lose your hair, oh where, oh where,
Oh, where does it go?
"I fly upon the wind and drift through
    the air
Until at last, I come to rest everywhere!"

Hold up one hand; extend and flutter fingers.
Blow lightly on fluttering fingers.

Drop fingers one by one; flutter hand behind back.

Flutter fingers of other hand overhead.
*Flutter fingers of both hands around; come to rest
    with sleeping gesture and big sigh.*

The Golden Boat

This is the boat, the golden boat,	*Cup hands together; rock hands.*
That sails the silver sea,	*Move hands in wave motion.*
These are the oars of ivory white,	*Interlace fingers with palms up.*
That lift and dip, that lift and dip.	*Lower and raise interlaced fingers.*
These are the ten little Ferrymen,	*Show ten fingers.*
To take the oars of ivory white,	*Interlace fingers with palms up.*
That lift and dip, that lift and dip,	*Lower and raise interlaced fingers.*
That move the boat, the golden boat,	*Cup hands together; rock hands.*
Over the silver sea.	*Move hands in wave motion.*

At the Beach

Betty Jones

Build a sandcastle to the sky,	*Pat air; move hands upward.*
Make a moat so when waves roll by	*Make a big circle with arms in front of body.*
The castle will stand with its sandy wall	*Hold arms upright with fingertips touching.*
'Til high tide comes and then it will fall.	*Fingers flutter at rooftop, and slowly flutter downward to lap.*

The Sea

Here is the deep blue sea,	*Move hands in wave-like motion.*
Here is the boat and here is me,	*Keep waving one hand; raise other, wiggle thumb.*
And all the fishes down below,	*Wiggle fingers of wave-hand.*
Wriggle their tails and away they go!	*Hide wiggling hand behind back.*

Seashell Song

Betty Jones

Can you hear the sea's song in this little shell?	*Cup hands and place hands in lap.*
Hold it up to your ear and listen, listen well.	*Put cupped hands to ear; listen.*
Swish-shoo-ooh!	
The seashell's song is from the silvery sea,	*Lower cupped hands, sway them side to side.*
Where the waves roll in, wild and free.	*Make rolling wave motion with hands, moving in, then out.*
Swish-shoo-ooh!	*Cup hands and place hands in lap.*
There upon the sand, the lovely seashell lies,	*Cup hands to heart.*
Until a little child finds this seaside prize.	
Swish-shoo-ooh!	*Cross hands at heart.*
So guard this shell, its life-long song,	
And remember the home where it belongs.	
Swish-shoo-ooh!	*Cup hands around mouth and voice loudly.*

The Tadpole

E. E. Gould

Underneath the water weeds,
Small and black I wriggle,
And life is most surprising,
Wiggle, waggle, wiggle.
There's every now and then a most
Exciting change in me,
I wonder, wiggle, waggle,
What I shall turn out to be?

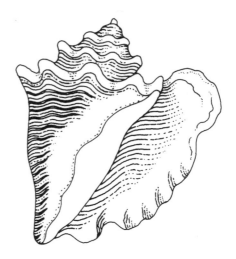

Summer Games

Red Light, Green Light

Children line up in a row. Light child is a number of yards away and stands turned away from the other children. Light child says, "Green Light!": children move towards Light as fast as they can until Light says, "Red Light!" and quickly turns back around to face children. Children must freeze in their places at this signal. If they move, they must return to the starting line. The child who reaches the Light first becomes the new Light and the game begins again.

Birds Fly

One child is chosen to come in front of the group and calls out a continuous stream of creatures, "Ducks fly, bees fly, horses fly," etc. If the creature mentioned does fly, the group goes through the motion of flying. If the creature does not fly, the group must stop, even if the leader continues speaking. Those children that fly when they should not are out. If many children are standing after a long time, leader chooses a replacement. Or, if there is only one child left, that child becomes the new leader.

Butterfly

Betty Jones

Dancing among the flowers with dainty painted wings
Flits the golden butterfly, joy to my heart she brings,
Stopping only for a rest to sip the morning dew,
Then flits and flutters off again—
Butterfly, I can't catch you!

Children sit in circle with hands held up and cupped on top of head acting as flowers. Butterfly dances inside circle, flitting in and out of space between seated children. Butterfly stops behind one child in circle for rest, bends, and sips dew by tickling a flower in child's palms. Flower child jumps up and chases butterfly back to his place, then becomes the next butterfly. Repeat game with the new butterfly.

Over the Hills and Far Away

Traditional, words and music

T-om h-e w-as a - pip-ers son. He learned t-o pl-ay wh-en he was young. And

a - ll th-e tu-ne th-at he could play was o - ver the hills a - nd far a - way.

O - ver the hills and a great way off, the wind shall blow m-y top - knot off.

2) Tom with his pipe made such a noise
   That he pleased both the girls and boys
   Who always stopped to hear him play
   Over the hills and far away!
   Over the hills and a great way off
   The wind shall blow my topknot off.

Standing in circle, children hold hands high singing while Tom skips, weaving in and out between them. At "The wind shall blow" Tom gently taps a child on the head to chase him around the circle while he runs to the child's place; that child becomes the new Tom and the game continues.

Summer Art and Handwork

Nature's Treasure Hunt

Go on as many outdoor adventures as possible and wherever you go hunt and gather nature's treasure (shells, feathers, pine cones, fallen bark, nutshells, acorn heads, wood chips, sticks, rocks) to create imaginative objects and landscapes to play in with grass dolls, fairies, and gnomes.

Tiny Terrarium

MATERIALS: Baby food jars, charcoal, extra soil and pebbles

PROCEDURE: While on a woodland walk, gather some of the following: mosses, lichens, tiny low-growing plants, pebbles, acorn, twigs, etc. Place a layer of pebbles and charcoal on the bottom of the baby food jar, then soil on top. Now arrange the woodland treasures. Water and cover with plastic wrap. Plants will survive indefinitely if kept moist.

Grass Dolls

While on a walk in an open field, the children can gently pull out a clump of dead tall grass, roots and all. Turn upside down and the roots become the hair. Tie at the neck with a strong piece of grass, raffia, or thread. Take another smaller clump of grass without roots and pass under the neck midway for arms. Tie under arms at waist to secure, and tie at each end of arms to indicate hands. Divide at waist remaining strands of grass, and tie at feet for legs or leave hanging as skirt.

Sand Painting

MATERIALS: Construction paper, plastic bags, beach sand (dark, light, coarse, and fine grain), shell pieces, glue

PROCEDURE: Collect small shell pieces and various colors and textures of sand in plastic bags. Children drizzle or brush glue on paper and sprinkle sand on top or arrange shell pieces. Let dry before lifting paper and allowing excess sand to fall off. Encourage children to use all colors and textures of sand on their painting to experience the differences visually and tactilely.

No-Sew Flying Fairy

MATERIALS: Fabric (fine cotton, silk, or satin) or tissue paper, fleece or cotton batting, string, stick, scissors

PROCEDURE: Cut a large diamond shape from pastel-colored fabric or tissue. Center a firm ball of fleece or cotton batting in the fabric for the head and tie firmly at the neck with string; let the material drape naturally. For hands, tie a knot at each of two opposite corners of the diamond. Take one of the two remaining unknotted corners and drape it over the fairy's head as if it were a hood; allow the pointed corner to form a bib end an inch or two below the fairy's neck (this forms the wings). Tie off as before at neck to secure with a string long enough to attach to a stick. Tie fairy to stick and let fly! You can also attach the knotted hands to the same stick so that the wings and arms remain outstretched.

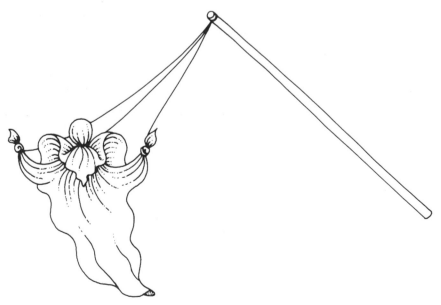

A Child's Seasonal Treasury

Summer Cooking and Baking

Summertime Picnic

Fruits and vegetables
  in season
Lemon juice
Cottage cheese

Whole-grain crackers
Cream cheese to spread
  (if desired)

With the children, peel, core, pit, and cut bite-sized pieces of summer fruits (apples, melons, strawberries, grapes, cherries, bananas, etc.) and place in bowl. To preserve color, squeeze a bit of lemon juice over cut fruit and mix through. In a separate bowl, prepare vegetable sticks (carrots, celery, cucumber, etc.). In a basket pack plates, napkins, and eating and serving utensils. Carry picnic basket to desired location, and when ready to eat, make sure children's hands are clean. They will prepare their own plate with a serving-spoonful of cottage cheese in the center, and a sunburst of fruit and vegetables around the cottage cheese, arranged to their tastes. Crackers can be passed around with cream cheese to spread on top.

Fruit Shake

2 cups cold juice (orange,
  pineapple, apple, grape)
1/2 cup powdered milk

Dash vanilla
Crushed ice

In a 1-quart container with a well-fitting cover, combine first three ingredients. Add the ice to the mixture and shake vigorously until smooth. Alternatively, you may combine all ingredients in a blender and blend until smooth.

Snow Cones

Juice (any flavor)
Crushed ice
Straws

Give each child a paper cup to scoop up crushed ice. Have them pack down their ice, and pour the juice over the ice to drink through a straw or slurp directly from the cup.

Peanut Butter Cookies

1 cup peanut butter
1/2 cup honey
1/2 cup oil (peanut, sesame, or canola)

1/2 tablespoon vanilla
1/4 tablespoon sea salt
2 cups whole wheat flour

Cream together the first three ingredients. Blend in vanilla and sea salt. Add flour a little at a time and mix well. Form the dough into balls and place on an oiled cookie sheet, flattening each ball with a fork. Bake for about 10 minutes in a preheated 350° F oven, watching closely to avoid burning. Makes about 2 1/2 dozen cookies.

Apricot-Almond Bake

1 1/2 cups dried apricots, chopped
1 1/2 cups boiling water
2 tablespoons sugar
1 teaspoon salt

1 1/2 cups whole wheat flour
1 tablespoon baking soda
1 cup unbleached white flour
1 cup chopped almonds
1 egg

In a large bowl, mix apricots, boiling water, sugar, and salt. Sift together whole wheat flour and baking soda, and add to apricot mixture. Mix well. Add white flour, nuts, and egg to other ingredients. Mix well and spread into greased oblong baking pan. Bake in preheated 350° F oven for 1 1/2 hours. Cool before cutting into squares.

Resources

Recommended Reading

Parenting and Early Childhood Theory

You Are Your Child's First Teacher, Rahima Baldwin
  (Celestial Arts, 1989)

Childhood: A Study of the Growing Soul, Caroline Von
  Heydebrand (Anthroposophic Press, Inc., 1995)

The Kingdom of Childhood, Rudolf Steiner (Anthroposophic
  Press, Inc., 1988)

The Way of a Child, A.C. Harwood (Rudolf Steiner Press, 1988,
  out of print)

Miseducation: Preschoolers at Risk, David Elkind (Knopf, 1987)

Raising a Daughter, Jeanne & Don Elium (Celestial Arts, 1994)

Raising a Son, Don & Jeanne Elium (Celestial Arts, 1987)

Lifeways: Working with Family Questions, edited by Gundrun
  Davy & Bons Voors (Hawthorne Press, 1993)

*Who's Bringing Them Up? Television and Child Development: How
  to Break the T.V. Habit,* Martin Large (Hawthorne Press, 1990)

Activities

Earthways: Simple Environmental Activities for Young Children,
  Carol Petrash (Gryphon House, 1992)

Festivals Together: A Guide to Multi-Cultural Celebration, Diana
  Carey & Judy Large (Hawthorne Press, 1993)

Festivals, Family, and Food, Diana Carey & Judy Large
  (Hawthorne Press, 1982)

The Children's Year, Stephanie Cooper, Christine Fynes-Clinton,
  & Marye Rowling (Hawthorne Press, 1990)

The Christmas Craft Book, Thomas Berger (Floris Books, 1986)

The Easter Craft Book, Thomas and Petra Berger (Floris
  Books, 1986)

The Harvest Craft Book, Thomas Berger (Floris Books, 1992)

*The Nature Corner: Celebrating the Year's Cycle with a Seasonal
  Tableau,* M. Leeuwen & J. Moeskop (Floris Books, 1990)

Painting with Children, Brunhild Müller (Floris Books, 1987)

Music and Poetry

*Kindergarten Books: Spring; Summer; Autumn; Winter; Spindrift;
  & Gateways,* compiled and written by Margaret Meyerkort
  (Wynstones Press, 1983)

Finger Plays for Nursery and Kindergarten, Emilie Poulsson
  (Dover, 1971)

The Laughing Baby, Remembering Nursery Rhymes and Reasons,
  Anne Scott (Bergin & Garvey, 1988)

Fairy Tales

*The Uses of Enchantment: The Meaning and Importance of Fairy
  Tales,* Bruno Bettelheim (Random, 1989)

The Poetry and Meaning of Fairy Tales, Rudolf Steiner (*out
  of print*)

The Complete Grimm's Fairy Tales, Jacob Grimm & Wilhelm K.
  Grimm. Edited by James Stern (Pantheon Books, 1976)

Catalogs

Creative Play

HearthSong: A Catalog for Families. Toys, art and craft supplies,
  beeswax, costumes, doll-making kits, and books. 156 North
  Main Street, Sebastopol, CA 95472, (800) 325-1525

Nova: Natural Family Store. Toys, Stockmar art supplies, silk
  scarves and capes, modeling beeswax and crayons, harps,
  and books. 817 Chestnut Ridge Road, Chestnut Ridge, NY
  10977, (914) 426-3757

Turtle Moon. Natural fiber costumes, silks, dolls, kits, books, and
  craft supplies. P.O. Box 161, Bodega, CA 94922,
  (707) 829-6732

Community Playthings. Large, sturdy wooden toys, kitchen sets,
  etc. P.O. Box 901, Rifton, NY 12471, (800) 777-4244

Heartwood Arts. Wooden castles, gnome houses, etc.
  15 TriBrook Road, Hillsdale, NY 12529, (800) 488-9469

Choroi. Beautiful instruments: lyres, kinderharps, chimes,
  violins, drums, bells, pentatonic and diatonic flutes. Karen
  and Peter Klaveness, 4600 Minnesota Avenue, Fair Oaks, CA
  95628, (916) 966-1227

Anthroposophic Press, Inc. Catalog. RR4, Box 94 A1, Suite 8,
  Hudson, NY 12534, (518) 851-2054

Specialty Craft Suppliers

Magic Cabin Dolls. Large selection of doll kits, supplies, and
  ready-made soft dolls. P.O. Box 64, Viroqua, WI 54665,
  (608) 637-2735

A Real Doll. Darian Dragge, Soft Doll and toy supplies and kits.
  P.O. Box 1044, Sebastopol, CA 95472, (707) 823-5370

Earth Guild. Supplies for spinning, weaving, dyeing, and
  basketry. 33 Haywood Street, Asheville, NC 28801,
  (800) 327-8448

Dharma Trading Company. Wool batting, roving, yarn, 100% cotton clothing for dyeing, textile supplies. P.O. Box 150916,
  San Rafael, CA 94915, (800) 542-5227

Weleda. Natural health care products, newsletter. P.O. Box 249,
  Congers, NY 10920, (914) 268-8599

School Supplies and Furniture

Mercurius School and Art Supplies. Wool felt, Stockmar beeswax,
  crayons, and watercolor paints. 7426 Sunset Avenue, Fair
  Oaks, CA 95628, (916) 863-0411

Sureway Trading Enterprises. Silk at very low prices. 826 Pine
  Avenue, Suites 5 & 6, Niagara Falls, NY 14301,
  (716) 282-4887

Index of First Lines

Subject and Title Index